County,

kind of a love story

County,
kind of a love story

Rebecca Wurtz

NINE BEAN ROWS

PRESS

ISBN 978-0-615-36589-3

Cover design by Ariel Miller

Cover photo © by David Kohrman

For Jeff

TABLE OF CONTENTS

County Hospital: told in rhyme   1

July first   5

County is the people's palace   14

George: every problem, many times   22

Less than nothing left for a thief   28

Women and Children's   35

All of us doctors in training   39

"AIDS is bad, cancer is badder"   43

You can complain or you can do   48

An obsolete parsimony   54

Plague upon plagues   59

Every available inch of space   62

David Tweedle   68

Chicago, known for big shoulders   72

A little mouse in no hurry   77

County belongs to the public   79

Ramadan   88

David and Jacek   93

This morning, things are looking grim   96

Christmas party   103

A new year, new leaf   109

Tuberculosis quarantine   116

Camino ciego   120

Protest March   126

Not all patients have infections   133

Failing TB treatment   137

Now, more than ever   143

Hansens   146

Oh vida por vivir y ya vivida   151

ACTG   157

Jacek goes home   160

Shanti's baby   163

Fools in the rain   167

Grace   175

June's last day   180

County Hospital: told in rhyme

Each fingertip, blue-black with ink,
is rolled on a card by a dour
civil servant who smells of drink.
My picture is taken before
a background of height hash marks, dead
on and profile. At each stop, I
sign my name and am waved ahead.
In the medical office, my
chest is quickly auscultated
to verify that my heart beats.
Three times, I am vaccinated.
The nurse motions with a cup, seats
herself, so that she can watch me
in the toilet stall while I pee.

What *is* this process, part booking,
part travel clinic? A newly
certified MD, I'm looking
for employment with the County.
A stack of forms is handed
to me, and I am out on Clark
Street, elated. I have landed
the job I want, at a landmark
institution. I start next week
at the Cook County Hospital,
storied, vast, decrepit, antique.
Once celebrated and vital,
now still needed, but ossified,
its missteps widely vilified.

It's a hospital in trouble:
an outmoded physical plant,
bureaucracy, inscrutable
finances, political cant.
A job at the County would be
punishment for some, daunting, foreign. In my chosen specialty,
the County's shortcomings are more
an opportunity. For me,
the chance to learn, to see, redeems
the place. So my visit to the
County Building is both, it seems,
booking for incarceration
and a long trip's embarkation.

My chosen field of medicine?
I am an infectious disease
doctor, a sub-specialist in
germs, contagion, and remedies.
The mellifluous Linnaean
bacterial taxonomy
and the challenging protean
exchange between humanity
and microbe affirm that ID
is medicine's canonical
field, its most noble specialty,
the synthesis of medical
sciences, arts, and history.
And lately, it has HIV.

In the early 1990s,
which is when this story is set,
AIDS is still a startling disease,
a wholly unexpected threat.
Just a couple decades before –
1969 – a near-sight-
ed leading public health doctor
declared that we had won the fight
against infectious disease. How
wrong he was! Just as I began
med school, AIDS erupted. By now
it had spread, faster, farther than
anyone could have predicted,
whole communities afflicted.

Lucky for me, every scourge,
given a chance, takes advantage
of natural law to emerge.
Bacteria "micro" manage
their evolutionary niche.
There will never *not* be new germs.
I will always have a job, which
HIV's existence confirms.
Zinsser wrote, "Infectious disease
is the last great adventure." Though
written in the 1930s,
the adventure is still real, nowhere more so than at Cook County.
It is the ID place to be.

"County?" My parents are appalled.
I grew up in the suburbs, where
"County" evokes fear. When I called
to tell them, my mom cried – I swear.
To be honest, I have only
the haziest idea of what
it is, a rudimentary
impression of Chicago's butt-
end, hulking on the evening news,
backdrop to inner city war-
fare and decay, a yellow bruise
fading to gray. The night before
I start, I'm as scared as a fey
candy striper on her first day.

4

July first

I get an office in what was
once the nurses' dormitory.
A desk. A folding chair because
that's all there is. Pretty sorry.
The division secretary,
Florida, suggests that I check
the loading dock for broken free
chairs. I find a rusted gooseneck
lamp, a desk chair missing a wheel,
easily fixed by a hardware
store trip, a caster, and some steel
wool. Soon I have a desk, a chair,
a light. I hang my diplom-
a. It begins to feel like home.

A colleague stops to say hello
and at noon escorts me to our
weekly division meeting. So
I meet Doctors Marks, El-Akbar,
Kralovec, and O'Connor. My
division chairman, my new boss,
regards me with a gimlet eye.
He's curdled now by time and loss,
but once had a promising career.
County taught him to avoid work,
has given him the thick veneer
of a lifer: the shrug, the smirk.
His only purpose seems to be,
at least today, impressing me.

His attitude is *laissez-faire*
toward how I fulfill my duties.
Sour: "As I'm sure you're aware,"…
pompous pause…"one of the beauties
of working here is, at County,
little is expected." Blink, yawn.
"You should try to be here every
week day, but seeing patients on
the weekend is…not required."
He pares his nails with a jackknife.
"Don't worry, you can't be fired…
at the County, you're here for life."
This isn't what I want to hear.
I am still earnest, young, sincere.

I want to believe that I will
not only be responsible
but necessary to cure ill-
ness, even indispensible.
Dr. Boss pontificates, "I'm
closing in on a cure for AIDS.
As a result, I don't have time
to see patients. I'll make some trades
with you on service." What a jerk!
I see now how it's going to be.
He wants me to do all his work.
He thinks I'll be his scut puppy.
I think he'll be my albatross.
His gain of time will be my loss.

How can I rescue the world while
baby-sitting for Dr. Boss?
Well, screw him! He'll hide in exile,
lounging in his lab, doing cross-
word puzzles for all I care. Four
years of medical school and six
years of training have made me more
than qualified to find and fix
County's patients' problems. Surely,
I'm ready to cure, given time,
the world's ills: disease, poverty,
maybe, someday, HIV. I'm
poised to cure all humanity,
if Dr. Boss will only let me.

On my second day, I am in
charge of the Infectious Disease
Consult Service. Adrenaline
covers for lack of expertise
as I display a confidence
I do not feel. Maybe four years
of school, six years in residence
was not really enough. These fears
dry my mouth and moisten my palms.
The team members of the service
wait, anticipating. My qualms
have triggered sporadic nervous
cardiac extrasystoles,
hyperhidrosis, shaking knees.

What do ID doctors do? We
see the patients whose infections
perplex their doctors. An MD,
if well-trained (with few exceptions),
knows how to diagnose and treat
routine complaints. When the problem
is rare or complex, lacks a neat
answer, is an odd exanthem,
puzzles the rheumatologists,
concerns a skin test reactor,
or, despite good treatment, persists,
an infectious disease doctor
gets involved. ID's bottom line?
If it ends in "itis," it's mine.

Let me put consults in context
also: who we are, what we do.
Members change monthly. For the next
four weeks, the team consists of two
doctors-in-training, Tranh and Lee;
Jack, a student; me. The group spends
all day rounding, reluctantly.
Our actual schedule depends
on the number of new consults' –
new patients' – histories, exams,
x-rays, smears, cultures, lab results,
and electrocardiograms
we perform, review, and discuss.
We sometimes spend an hour thus.

An hour for *each* new patient
that is, and a few minutes for
each of the "old" ones. Efficient
we are not. Dr. O'Connor
handed the "service" over to
me last evening. It took him three
hours to discuss and review
forty plus patients he "gave" me.
If we talk to, examine, and
discuss each case, plus work and write
up new consults…Oh, God, I've planned
enough to keep us here all night!
I feel like I'll regurgitate.
"I'm the new doctor. Am I late?"

Hours of rounds, borborygmi.
It's one o'clock. We've "rounded on"
fifteen patients, with thirty-three
more to visit. Surrounded on
all sides by questions, updates, calls,
new consults, old problems, I feel
like I'm juggling four dozen balls,
sliding on a banana peel.
We pause for ten minutes for lunch.
This is good because I must look
up some smart answers to a bunch
of questions. I skim my textbook.
What's – swallowing my sandwich whole –
the dose for thiabendazole?

Regrouping, we've found our second
wind. We stop to see a pregnant
teen, her TB slow to respond,
an Asian man with fulminant
meningitis, a not-quite healed
bedsore, a comatose fellow
stabbed in the chest at Wrigley Field
(the top of the 8th), with yellow
jaundice. Four beds down lies the man
who stabbed him – beaten, killed almost,
by his bleeding victim. He began
running a fever three days post
admission. Cops sit with each guy:
under arrest, unless they die.

The last consult of the day proves
to be most difficult, at least
diagnostically. It behooves
me to be right: a crowd has eased
in around the consult team to
hear my discussion on a man
with Reiter's or DGI, two
conditions which look alike. Tranh
presents the patient's story. Young
black male, twenty-two, seven days
of joint aches, fever, tender tongue,
maybe some red eyes, mild malaise.
No past or family histories.
No meds, no food/drug allergies.

Two days ago, on arrival,
oral temp one hundred point three,
possibly some conjunctival
inflammation, swollen right knee
and wrist. Lab tests unrevealing,
he was treated for DGI
and Reiters, both, with quick healing.
Now afebrile, joint pain gone. "My
knee's all better, doc, can I go?"
That would be fine with me, but his
primary service needs to know:
if I had to make a choice, is
this guy's problem DGI or
Reiters? I am the arbiter.

The "right" diagnosis is moot:
he's been treated and is now cured.
He can go home; there's no dispute.
It's peace of mind they want, insured
only if we give it a name.
Doctors need to categorize,
to ease each case into a frame-
work, a pattern we recognize.
The "real" diagnosis? I don't know.
But in order to slide one's mind
smoothly past a case, to let go,
we need a place where it's assigned.
So, I designate DGI
and summarize my reasons why.

People relax. They murmur "thank
you," not because I got it "right"
but because I've filled in the blank.
Although it's 8 o'clock at night
interns and residents hurry
back to work. The Admitting Ward
frantically pages Tranh and Lee:
nine admissions are on the board
and they're on call tonight. They dart
off. I set the dazed student free
and finish alone. For my part,
I am amazed. I'm amazed because when *I* gave that case a name –
DGI – that's what it became.

My memories of the next few
weeks commingle like the crusted
rivulets formed when "dew,"
condensing on County's rusted
steam pipes in basement corridors
drips and is channeled into ruts
gouged in ancient cement floors.
We saw so many patients. What's
more: I saw diseases that I'd
only read about in books. Who
knew that on Chicago's west side
time and place would be so askew?
Old and third world diseases might
thrive within the Sears Tower's sight?

Our patients' woes – like tetanus –
should be ten thousand miles away
or – like bleak tuberculosis –
decades ago, not here, today.
I would have been more lost than I
was without Florida. She taught
me how to fill out forms, found my
stethoscope (I mislaid it), brought
me coffee early one morning
(she caught me asleep at my desk),
issued a friendly forewarning
about our sometimes Kafkaesque
crises. "Don't waste time trying to
explain County's failings. Just do."

County is the people's palace

Public hospitals tend to be
magnificent edifices.
Bellevue, Bart's, Bulfinch, Charity.
Only the ornate suffices.
It's as if the municipal
fathers assuage their civic guilt
by building the grandiose shell
of a public trust. Having built
the granite metaphorical
and literal façades of care,
they are absolved, historical-
ly, of the burdensome nightmare,
that nagging and ongoing need:
providing care in stone *and* deed.

Like many of Cook County's deals,
building County proved a feedlot
for those whose friendships greased the wheels.
An alderman's son-in-law got
the architect's job, a brother
the plumbing. Wiring, roof, mas-
sonry by one pal or other.
County admitted its first case
in 1914. The "People's
Palace" is an imposing pile,
one of the last few examples
of Chicago's late Beaux Arts style.
A palace of the people, sure,
the people with a sinecure.

At its debut, the main entrance
was its most remarkable space.
Two stories, with an abundance
of fine ornament, a showplace.
Marble benches, an inlaid floor,
later murals and mosaics
depicting County's open door.
A well-spring for the esthetics
of public design at the dawn
of the twentieth century.
Entering patients must have drawn
strength, seeing their community
make a pledge to their well-being
and, in granite, guaranteeing.

Carved into the marble, Pasteur's
noble promise has sentiments
that I will paraphrase. You're
welcome, whatever accidents
of fate have brought you here. Nation
and religion? Ethnicity, race?
Wealth or none? We do not question
someone who suffers in this place.
We merely say, you suffer.
You are in pain, injured, ill.
You are sick. That is enough for
me. Your problem is mine. I will
do my best to treat your illness, soothe
your pain, clear your mind, help you breathe.

This portal (and that promise) has
deteriorated with time,
marble replaced by crummy plas-
tic chairs and linoleum. Grime,
not grout, cements broken floor tiles.
Mythic mural paint is peeling.
Decades-old graffiti defiles
an acoustic tile dropped ceiling.
The once majestic entrance now
does not reassure, resembling
more a laundromat. And the vow
carved sincerely, no dissembling,
promised by Pasteur as proxy?
Gone, its grooves filled with epoxy.

I've talked about the history
of the building. But what about
the people? The employees, the
patients, the visitors – without
people animating the place,
County is a curiously
melancholy and soulless space.
(And if you ask, suspiciously,
how I know what the hospital
is like without the people, I'll
tell you of my sentimental
visit to the abandoned pile,
become a *memento mori*
some ten years after this story.)

On this hot August day the halls
and wards are thronged with a thousand
people, sick and well. A nurse calls
patients' names. A hawker sells sand-
wiches to the people who wait
all day in the clinic to be seen.
By the desk, a patient, irate,
chews out a clerk, yelling "Sixteen?
Sixteen?" The hubbub is chronic.
Thousands work here, some sincerely.
One thousand visit the clinic,
six hundred in-patients, nearly
five hundred come to the ED
every single day at County.

Albert Poisson runs this place, or
tries to. His nickname, Big Possum,
springs from his style as director:
1) a habit of post-mortem-
like rigidity when challenged,
and 2) hiding during daylight.
He and the hospital have changed
in the decades since his first night
as a diener in the morgue. But
BP knows Cook County backward
and forward and that's really what
counts, not the fact the County Board
president is his cousin. He's
touchy though; don't mention that. Please.

Employees are a diverse band.
All races can be found, although
most doctors are white, like me, and
nurses black or Filipino.
Most come from the same places, so
speak the same languages County's
patients speak: Spanish, Urdu, Polish, Lao, Bridgeport, AAVEse,
a polyglot consortium.
All origins, ethnicities,
economic strata; in sum,
complexity like the city's.
As a group, we have one shared tic:
we tend to vote Democratic.

Most of the patients are black. Why?
Half the people in Chicago
are black. They get sicker and die
faster than white folks, doing so
without the benefit of private health insurance, so clearly
a factor. Immigrants supply
a second group, especially
those without a community
tightly-knit. Third: people who can't
succeed in life's society.
The mentally ill, the vagrant,
even someone, illiterate,
who can't tell time and shows up late.

As for visitors: very few.
The staple of most hospital
stays – the kind but awkward guest, who
starts leaving upon arrival?
Rare at County. It's hard to park,
even harder to take the El
or bus here. Patient wards are dark,
noisy, overheated. They smell.
Visitors have no bedside space
to sit (no chairs) or put flowers.
County's not a welcoming place,
even at visiting hours.
Still not clear why no one visits?
Let me paint you some ward portraits.

The patient "rooms" at the County
are traditional Nightingale
wards: long, narrow, open, twenty
beds on each side. At one time, male
and female patients were confined
to separate wards. Now curtains
and flimsy half-walls are combined
to separate them. This maintains
an illusion of privacy.
The wards have open windows, fans,
and small "dirty" utility
rooms for used meal trays and bedpans.
Solariums remain from the
time when sun was salutary.

But since sun is no longer deemed
healthy, these rooms are crowded with
beds. Patients aren't restored, they're steamed
when the sun reaches its zenith.
At the head of the ward, where it
joins the main building, the ward clerk
sits, imposing, as would befit
the empress of the realm of work.
The clerk potentate: Miss Mabley
Imperturbable, despotic.
She prefers "just Mabley." Frankly,
to challenge her is quixotic.
Nothing goes – no test or transfer –
sans Just Mabley's imprimatur.

The people's palace? Sure, if white
bread packaged as a single slice
in a cellophane wrapper might
be considered a royal vice.
If you have ever had to stay
in the hospital, you know that
the day's highlight is the food tray.
I'm being really diplomat-
ic when I say that few patients
at County ever awaited
their trays with pleasure. Ambience-
free, processed, canned, packed, past-dated,
meals are utilitarian,
suitably proletarian.

Wards' high ceilings and ancient light
fixtures lend an air of vintage
charm, which I guess would be all right
if quaintness were an advantage.
This covers – oh, did I forget?
We – I'll try to be delicate –
haven't talked about toilets yet.
At County, there are no private
bathrooms. The amenities, then:
dorm-style toilets, showers, and sinks.
One is for men, one for women,
and one for clerks, lest someone thinks
members of the ruling classes
don't have special ruling asses.

George: every problem, many times

A Chicago summer weekend.
No air conditioning, few fans.
Ragged screens let fly gangs descend
on overflowing garbage cans.
Since there are not enough nurses,
most patients haven't bathed in days.
Used bed linen intersperses
with uncollected dinner trays.
The people's palace? Only if
a palace smells like rotten food
and melena. A face-smack whiff
hits me hard on a Sunday you'd
swear was concocted in Hades.
High 100, low: the 80s.

For this month, I am assigned to
the AIDS Consult Service. We try
to see all the in-patients who
are HIV positive. Why?
In the early 1990s,
incurable, untreatable,
HIV is a dread disease,
and its victims forgettable.
Sometimes patients are neglected,
complex problems misunderstood.
We make sure that they're connected,
that their doctors do what they should.
We cross the "t's" and dot the "i's,"
put out fires as needs arise.

(I write "untreatable" but in
fact, there were two medications:
AZT, blue and white, taken
without fail, no hesitations,
every 4 hours. Even at
3 am, people rise from sleep
to take it. At times, I thought that
some stayed awake, to brood or weep.
The only other, DDI,
had its own peculiar aspects.
Taking one or both meds might buy
some time, but both had side effects
which seemed, to many, to outweigh
benefits of disease delay.)

The County's AIDS Service has two
residents, the med student, me,
plus the HIV RN, Lu.
Luis is the one constancy
on the service, month in, month out.
Lu is handsome, light-hearted, gay.
The patients adore him, no doubt
in part because, "like us," they say,
Lu is HIV positive.
He doesn't make it a big deal.
The fact that he is so alive
inspires the patients who feel
their lives have ended with the news
of AIDS and the fates it construes.

Lu dances through the day, music
playing in his head, short dreads bob-
bing to idiosyncratic
melodies. This nurse loves his job!
He would, and does, give his last dime
to patients in need of the pay
phone. Luis always makes the time
to sit, to talk, explain, convey,
listen to complaints. His gracious,
joking playfulness gains the trust
of even the most suspicious.
As we sweat our way through August,
the consult service census climbs.
Many patients, not enough dimes.

The sickest AIDS patients often
have a problem more than once. So
it is with this consult. Listen
as I put my stethoscope to
his chest: bilateral Velcro.
Oxygen 40, blue nail beds,
6th time, unbelievable, so
out of choices and out of meds.
"George, it's likely pneumocystis."
Gasping breaths, a small smile. "That's…fun."
A minute later, the nurse, pissed:
"He's refusing intubation."
The ICU transfer I've signed
in hand, I go to change his mind.

"You don't know – I don't think you see.
You might collapse, you might succumb – "
George cuts me off. "It's PCP.
And I will die…I'm sick, not dumb…
I'm tired of being a poor
man with AIDS…of standing in eight
hour lines…for pills that don't cure
me…that just make me retch…I hate
needles…I hate being afraid
of…this. Each time is…like…drowning.
…No tube. My decision is made."
I stand by his head, my frowning
face hidden from his eyes, weighing
words. I heard what George was saying.

He was choosing to die. I, new
doctor, lacked his ability,
his judgment, and his resolve to
give up his life so gracefully.
The nurse was young and new like me.
I asked her if she was okay
if we gave George morphine to decrease air hunger. She did not say,
but her eyes met mine and she drew
the syringe. We started with four
and moved to ten. His chest flew
up and down at first, then more
slowly, and he smiled, settled, stayed.
George had choices: the one he made.

His nurse and I took turns. Luis
came to sit with us, with George. He
recounted how George was at peace
at last clinic's visit. Clearly,
though not without sorrow or tears,
George eulogized his diminished
life. He accepted his long years'
illness, but said he was finished.
This time, he held himself under
and made himself drown. The blood-dark
froth spilled from his mouth. My wonder
at his bravery and my stark,
sheer insignificance collide.
I sat with him until he died.

I return to my office tired
and sad. What does it mean to be
a doctor when all that's required,
all you can do, is…nothing? We
spend, in school, so much time learning
to do…something. Learning to do
nothing is hard: no discerning,
labs, or formulas to guide you.
Still more surprising to me: the
effort it takes to underpin
doing nothing. Elzbieta,
his nurse. Luis. George. Imagine.
A few weeks ago, it was me
whom I thought so necessary.

My telephone rings and I pick
it up. A woman's urgent plea:
"Doctor, doctor, come quick, come quick!"
She hangs up. Oh, great. Who was she?
This has happened once before, when
I was working late. A woman
called, quite frantic, asked for help, then
hung up. At the time I didn't plan
for it to happen again. I
call the switchboard operator,
but she can't determine who my
caller might be. They want me for
what? Where are they calling from? Why?
I can't guess so I can't reply.

Less than nothing left for a thief

The handsome surgeon pulls out my
chair at a steakhouse in the Loop.
I suggested a fish place – I
don't like steak. I'll just order soup.
I'd gone out once or twice with this
man before I started at County, but
since then, I haven't returned his
calls. "It's so easy to get in a rut,
you know, when you're busy," I say
sweetly, opening the menu.
We order, and he leans in. "Okay,
why go to work at County? Who
are the patients? Don't all of them
have AIDS? I've heard the place's mayhem."

I tell him about the County's
roots, the wards, the food, courageous
George, Luis', BP's, Just Mabley's
stories, funny, sad, outrageous.
"You can't generalize about
the people at County. Some work
with vigor and kindness. Some flout
the mission of the place and jerk
the patients and the rest of us
around. Some people care fiercely,
and some not at all. The callous
and the caring at times scarcely
seem on the same plane. It's not what
I expected. It's much more, but..."

I think I'm doing a good job
explaining why County excites
me, until this would-be heartthrob
interrupts my paean. He cites
the reasons why County is ripe
for disdain. He starts with the staff
(mainly nurses), takes a sideswipe
at the patients, spends almost half
an hour trashing my future
and finishes, finally, by
deriding the doctors. "I'm sure
they couldn't get a job at my
hospital – that's why they work there,
servicing patients on welfare.

"Come on! You're wasting your training.
You could work at a prestigious
hospital. What are you gaining
there? It's disgusting, egregious."
In my mind I enumerate
the problems I've seen at County:
meds not given, inadequate
nurses, petty bureaucracy,
bad cafeteria food, flak-
ing paint, third world-type infection.
Clearly I have made a mistake,
I've made an unwise selection.
Not with County, but with this guy.
He made it easy to say goodbye.

To myself, I admit his pokes
draw blood. When I talk on the phone
with my med school classmates, their jokes
about County, the mocking tone,
make me wince. Repeatedly I'm
shocked by the tragicomedy
surrounding me. Most of the time,
patients get just one dose of three
that were ordered. One day last week,
an OR ceiling fell – collapsed
during a case – from a roof leak.
JCAH credentials lapsed,
and Medicare has us blackballed.
Federal reimbursement's stalled.

Despite all this (of which no one
is proud), patients keep coming. There's
no where else to go. That tension
sweeps us all along, daily bears
us up: there's no where else to go.
County is the frayed safety net,
preferable to an ice floe
but scarcely more humane. And yet
people keep coming. AIDS patients
capture it best: marginalized
before their illness, privations
I can't imagine. Pauperized
now, sick in ways that strain belief,
less than nothing left for this thief.

The AIDS Ward is on the 6th floor
of a separate building. We
trudge upstairs. The elevator
is broken again. We hardly
care, but the patients are stranded.
No tests today, no procedures.
Less work for us, I'll be candid:
no new admissions, no transfers.
Food trays and medicine are sent
up and down in a dumbwaiter.
Patients stay put. In the event
one dies, the body's moved later.
One elevator, one stairwell.
Escape plan for a fire? Hell.

Doctors and nurses carrying
patients to the roof to be plucked
by helicopters, ferrying.
Ice, wind, a raging storm? We're fucked.
The AIDS Ward, like all the others,
has two dozen beds, two dorm-style
toilets. It's the "band of brothers"
cohesion that makes it worthwhile.
We transfer all AIDS in-patients
here, if there is room on the Ward.
It isn't for our convenience.
Rather, so they won't be ignored.
AIDS patients are still stigmatized.
Their remains might be fossilized

long before they get attention
on the regular wards. Here we
provide respite, not to mention
fresh fruit, good coffee, sympathy.
The AIDS Ward has some rules: no guns,
no cursing, no party drugs, some
semblance of respect for everyone's
few square feet of space, refrain from
loud music and talking after
10 p.m. In return we get
to know families, patients' laughter;
a Christmas carolers' quartet;
visits from patients after they've
left, fly once they shower and shave.

The AIDS Ward has its regulars,
"frequent fliers" is what they're called.
To this day, their particulars
linger in my memory. Bald
Tavi, getting radiation
for Kaposi's. Cheerful Jerome,
in jail as much as out. Haitian
Tonton wants only to go home.
Cheeto, an albino black man,
has orange hair and freckles, a bad
temper, and a dextromorphan
addiction. Dante, Dennis, Brad
have STDs of various
types. Tattooed Bear, gregarious.

The nurses here are outstanding:
Elzbieta, Victor, Breeann.
The charge nurse, "old school"-demanding,
Mrs. Nenita Bigayan,
earned her nursing bachelor's degree
(Class of 1967,
Manila University)
before these nurses were even
born. No one knows why Mrs. B.
is the charge nurse for the AIDS Ward.
She has no special empathy,
no excess of compassion, toward
AIDS patients. She takes narrow views
of sex, drugs, and IVDUs.

Union rules and seniority
probably secured her this post.
The patients call her – because she
stands, in shoes, five feet tall (at most)
but looms over mischief makers –
Big Nurse. Mrs. Bigayan's sons
and husband are undertakers.
She must share their dispositions.
For a place where things rarely run
like clockwork, Mrs. Bigayan
and her nurses can get things done.
And even though their motives span
a range – efficiency versus
empathy – they're all great nurses.

Women and Children's

On Wednesdays, I work at the humble "Women and Children with AIDS Clinic." Women, moms, and kids come with so many needs, it evades comprehension. Gay men have built an alliance in response to AIDS. In protest, they've sewn a quilt. They support one another through illness and death. Now, compare that with the isolation felt by women with AIDS. Just a glance at these faces seems to verify how little the forty women waiting today have in common.

Some mill around talking, others hang
out at the clerk's desk, read to their
children, eat a sandwich, harangue
their boyfriends, or plead for bus fare.
Different risk factors, races,
ages. Prostitutes, drug addicts,
grandmothers. Far-advanced cases
and new diagnoses. What sticks
in my mind: most keep their status
secret, even from family.
Here in clinic, anonymous,
these women temporarily
belong to a community:
an HIV sorority.

W & C was started
and is led by Fran Campion,
a passionate, lion-hearted
internist and AIDS champion.
Fran is an irresistible,
uncompromising, potent force
against County's immovable,
inert mountain. A major source
of headaches for Big Possum, Fran
takes no prisoners. ("If you're not
for us, you're against us.") She can
be harsh, strident. Her scattershot
insults make me wary. The staff
takes pains to steer clear of her gaff.

The clinic manager, Grace, is
as cheerful and yielding as Fran
is intransigent. The basis
of her strength and effortless élan?
In a prior career, Grace was
a dancer, modern and ballet.
Now all the partners in her *pas*
de deux are patients. The *entrée:*
"You are welcome in our clinic."
Adagio: "Life is hard when
you have HIV. No picnic,
AIDS isn't. But you're here. Amen!
It took courage to come, I know."
Next: variations, to and fro.

"You sure you have enough money
for bus fare?" "For diapers?" "For heat?"
"How's your mom?" "Lookin' good, honey!"
At last, the *coda:* "Girl, I'm beat."
Grace alights for a second, then
jumps up to restock supply carts,
hand out crayons to the children,
help the clerk, Cassandra, file charts.
Lots of people with HIV/
AIDS did quite well, you might protest.
Yes, but this is County's story.
This is about the dispossessed.
Men and women starting with not
much found they still could lose a lot.

Besides Fran and me, there are three
other doctors: an internist,
a family doc, and an OB.
Residents and students assist.
We are the clinic collective!
One basic rule: everyone stays
until all are done, reflective
of our shared commitment. Long days
result. By the time I double
back to see any new consults,
check on old patients in trouble,
and follow up on lab results,
it's often 10 pm before
I drag through my apartment's door.

All of us doctors in training

Noon, the ID service, café-
teria. Since I cover for
Dr. Boss, I round every day.
I've gotten to know a lot more
of the residents than other
attendings. During lunch, interns
stop by, one after another,
with questions, new consults, concerns.
The members of the ID team
this month: Vikram, a resident
from Calcutta, and Ibrahim,
an intern from Iran. Intent
on getting back to work, we hunch
over our trays, hurrying lunch.

Care at County is provided
by young doctors-in-training, so-
called residents. They are guided
by attending doctors, although
some were respected, practicing
physicians in their home countries
prior to re-apprenticing
here. U.S. universities,
fifty years past, graduated
men vying for County training
because these jobs situated
a doctor for life, ordaining
for him a professional seat
among the medical elite.

Now American medical
graduates look down their noses
at County. Virtually all
house staff are foreign. This poses
language and culture gaps. Most are
conservative Muslims, Hindus.
They've lived, in miles and mindset, far
from homelessness, IV drug use,
and homosexuality.
And yet, despite the distance
they've come, they work tirelessly
to care for the County's patients.
They are ambitious, eager, smart,
but ask me, "What means this word 'fart'?"

On ID consults, although we
see a near-zoo – malaria,
tuberculosis, HIV,
cyclospora, filaria,
syphilis and gonorrhea,
encephalitis, PCP,
sepsis, measles, diarrhea,
cysticercosis, CMV –
on most days, it's not dramatic.
Mostly it's urine infections,
plain pneumonia, problematic
purulent (pus filled) collections,
antibiotic resistance,
unexplained fever persistence.

We're on the move all day, making
rounds, writing notes. Walking, I teach,
discussing the cases, taking
every patient as a text. Each
member of the team, depending
on his or her level – student,
resident, and yes, attending –
learns something. "What's the most prudent
antibiotic choice for this
newborn?" "What evidence suggests
Mrs. Chang has opisthorchis?"
"Pneumonia sometimes manifests
as torpor in the elderly,
as it has in Mr. Hurley."

To be honest, I learn from them
as much as I teach them. A case
of malaria prompts Vikram
to tell of poor mothers who race
with an unconscious child in their
arms 15, 18 – sometimes more –
kilometers on foot, seeking care
and quinine. He quotes from Tagore
for us: "devotion is beauty
itself." Ibrahim tells stories
about his medical duty
in Iran's war with Iraq. He's
reminded, he tells us, his face grim,
of mustard gas by a burn victim.

I take the team out to dinner
at the consult service month's end.
Though I pay, I'm the meal's winner,
terrific food my dividend,
plus the scoop on which places are
authentic. Tonight we're dining
at the Udupi Palace, our
conversation intertwining
travelogues, politics, and work.
This multi-nation consult crew
is yet another County perk,
expanding my diet world view
from local and pedestrian
to global epicurean.

"AIDS is bad, cancer is badder"

Dale is a middle age black man.
Longtime user, started smoking
at 12. At 40 he began
losing weight, thereby provoking
an AIDS eval. HIV was
almost a bye, the likelihood
was so high. Then panic, because
he had started coughing up blood.
My first thought: tuberculosis.
Weeks of tests to find the answer.
Dale's second bad diagnosis
was not TB but lung cancer.
So he's admitted, cachexic,
amiable, chatty, and sick.

The oncologists plan chemo
and radiation. Dale prizes
the radiation "tat" below
his right fourth rib. He surprises
me: it's the only tattoo he
ever got, despite his time in
Vietnam and jail. "Look at me!"
showing off the daub in his skin.
Dale loves to read, *noir* mysteries
mainly. He thumbs Elmore Leonard
at night in the toilet, carries
Cain whenever he leaves the Ward,
takes Mickey Spillane as a guide
on rambles for a smoke outside.

This morning, when I arrive for
rounds, the Ward's unusually
quiet, neither breakfast trays nor
morning meds passed yet. Everyone is sleeping in, except Dave
Tweedle, a man with dementia
who talks continuously. Grave,
humanity *in absentia*,
a housekeeper in a haz-mat
suit mops the men's toilet. The sea-
air tang of fresh blood gouges at
my nostrils. I look – warily –
in the call room. Residents slouch,
bleary-eyed, on the sagging couch.

Taj, the overnight intern, stood.
"Dale went to the bathroom, started
to cough, then spewed fountains of blood.
The nurse called me stat. I parted
the watchful, silent crowd, and found
poor Dale, dead, turned on his side, his
knees pulled up. Blood-soaked on the ground
beside was 'The Big Sleep.' What is
worse, the other patients were scared.
'Did HIV or cancer cause
Dale's death?' Lung cancer, I declared.
After only the slightest pause:
'Oh yeah, cancer is *bad*,' they said.
Thus reassured, they went to bed."

Dale, a sweetheart, in his maroon
pajamas and robe. I picture
him face down on the tile, book strewn,
his dimmed expression a mixture
of surprise and "what can you do?"
A week passes and I can't let
that image go. Both Grace and Lu
sit me down. "Don't think you'll forget
Dale, and don't think you failed him. He
would have needed a miracle.
Cancer *and* AIDS?! Seriously?
Now we're going to get personal,
though we don't mean to criticize.
You need sleep, girl. And exercise!"

Riding my bike on the lakefront
path, I witness a common sight,
a crash. A blader bears the brunt —
she's down, holding her ankle tight.
Another good Samaritan,
a cute guy riding a Trek bike,
and I stop to see if we can
help. The blader's up. It looks like
she's okay. The seriously cute
Samaritan's name is Will, and
we talk and flirt for a minute,
then two, then fifteen. On his hand,
when he pedals off, he's written
my name and phone number in pen.

A few days later, Will calls and
invites me to a gallery
opening in Bucktown. We stand
sipping wine, conversing shyly.
He runs ArtsLaw, a non-profit
group which helps artists navigate
IP rights, the laws which permit
creative people to create,
protect their ingenuity,
and maybe make a living. I'm
struck by the incongruity:
the painters' controlled and sublime
brushstrokes versus the bold slashes
of life and color County splashes.

We walk the few blocks to Lulu's
on Damen for dinner. Only
in Chicago: Thai food and blues
music. "I've heard of Cook County
Hospital, but I don't know where
it is," Will laughs, "or what they – you –
do." Lack of knowledge isn't rare.
The river, Western Avenue,
County Hospital: some things just
keep going, whether people know.
Talking about work, art, life, trust.
Ideas, laughter overflow.
Over green curry and *pad se ew*,
we talk until it's almost two.

You can complain or you can do

There is never enough money
to run County. Tax dollars just
pay a fraction of each penny
spent. Also, because *someone* must,
a public hospital offers
health care services which don't earn
jack to fill for-profit coffers.
Special care such as trauma, burn,
and TB wards. Everyone who
needs unwonted care is happy
to find County exists, it's true.
Not as happy to *fund* County,
though, as they are quick to tell you
when property taxes are due.

What with politics, graft, listless
oversight, fiscal suspensions,
County is a financial mess.
Budgets are complete inventions,
bookkeeping appears spasmodic.
Full accounting? BP demurs.
Consequently episodic
odd scarcity sometimes occurs.
No isotope scans 'til the end
of next month; we are in arrears.
The gallium vendor won't send
more until County's check clears.
No clean gowns before Saturday.
No quinolones before next May.

At first I was outraged and scared.
I can't take care of patients if
I don't have the right tools. I shared
my grievance, a righteous plaintiff,
with anyone who would listen.
"How can you take care of patients
without a 'blank?'" (I'd fill it in
depending on the audience.)
Eventually, Fran pulled me
aside. "Get over it. We don't
always have what we want, but we
have what we need. Arguing won't
change that – it just wastes time. Figure
it out." I'm stung by her censure.

Stung but also frustrated and
confused by this repeated koan,
"Don't complain or gripe or grandstand.
Use your drive to do." I, alone,
seem angry, pissed off, wound up tight.
As natural as inhaling
to me is trying to make things right,
not accept the system's failing.
Why allow this misalignment
of social policies and needs?
There should be a reassignment
of money, resources, and deeds.
How to still my aggravation?
Here's today's interpretation:

Concentrate your mind on this man.
Everything you've got is right here,
right now. Do with it what you can,
for him. Do your best, persevere.
The sick man doesn't care about
mac- or microeconomics.
He just wants me to figure out
adequate antibiotics.
Instead of constant rearranging,
find the center, where it's quiet
and perhaps instead of changing
County, you will be changed by it.
Make things right with what you've got; this
patient, for now, is your focus.

The upside of inconstant re-
sources (at least from my point-of-view)
is that shortage requires me
to be smarter, to think things through.
If I can't get a certain med
I need to know its substitutes.
We're out of oral drug. Instead,
I have to give by other routes.
If I can't get a CT scan
on a patient for a week, I
need a new diagnostic plan.
No EKGs? What's my standby?
Stringency may make me better
but for the sick, lack's a fetter.

Meanwhile, an informal system
of barter and exchange abides.
This economy, an emblem
of ingenuity, provides
the surest way to acquire
anything from adding machines
to Zoloft. If you require,
say, a stapler, behind the scenes
you might go to someone who knows
what the going rate of exchange
is for office supplies. Suppose
I ask Florida the price range
for a stapler. She might ask Delnor who has a stapler to sell.

Del swaps a bassinet for six
typewriter ribbons. Florida
trades the crib to Pediatrics
for flu vaccine, because Frieda
in Pulmonary Medicine
has spare staples and a stapler
but has run out of the vaccine.
Got that? Nothing could be simpler.
Delnor works in Central Supply,
the storage room in the basement.
He is the built-big kind of guy
in body and soul, a servant
of the people to whom Pasteur
promised a welcome and succor.

Del's is the invisible hand
connecting needs with resources.
The wheels of supply and demand,
when Delnor and Flo join forces,
turn smoothly. Puts are his; calls, hers.
This underground economy
in their hands hums, warbles, and purrs.
Delnor supplies, while Flo – well, she
knows every one there is to know.
Best of all, she's sweet on Delnor.
Even better, Del's sweet on Flo.
Del loiters at the storeroom door
for Florida to "happen" by.
Florida "happens." She says hi.

Where other men might give flowers,
Delnor flirts with office supplies.
Florida herself spends hours
searching for *billet-doux* replies.
A cathode ray tube, Vero cells,
a Mayo clamp are her prized finds.
When I see Florida and Del's
free trade, I have hope for mankind's.
It was to Florida I turned
when I needed a new stapler.
From chits she'd previously earned
she bartered for one for me. Her
talent at finessing these deals
says more than her job title reveals.

An obsolete parsimony

I n medical school we were taught
the beauty of parsimony.
The differential refined thought.
Infinite possibility
was sharpened to its finest point,
a single determination.
Our learned goal was to anoint
the simplest interpretation,
one diagnosis as the cause,
a uniting judgment spoken.
Unfortunately, like most laws,
this one was made to be broken.
HIV blunts Occam's razor.
Four diagnoses don't amaze or

perturb me. AIDS patients often
have many problems at the same
time. Two newly diagnosed men,
young and away from home, will frame
this discussion. I recognize
the first patient, a busboy at
a restaurant I patronize,
a Mexican store front joint that
serves great *barbacoa*. He shows
no sign of knowing me. His Western blot was positive. This goes
along with the bronch and the rest
of his test results: PCP,
syphilis, and latent TB.

Lu and I have come to tell him.
I introduce myself; it's six
o'clock and the day has grown dim.
The October twilight plays tricks
with my eyes. Here, he looks more like
a child, a boy. He is heedless
of the blow, poised, about to strike.
I'm sorry to bear such distress.
My poor Spanish: *"Buenos tarda."*
Then the words no one wants to hear:
"Soy un medicade SIDA."
Luis helps make my meaning clear.
I ask the patient's permission
to sit with him. Intuition

tells me that we will need to take
some time here. We talk. His tears fall.
He looks as if his heart will break.
His name is Emanuel. "Call
me Mannie. Please." His father gone,
Mannie supports both his mother
and aunt in *Nuevo Leon*,
working full-time, plus another
job part-time. Mannie speaks in Span-
glish. Lu translates the interplay.
My Spanish is poor but I can
understand more than I can say.
I assure Mannie that we will
take care of him while he is ill.

When we see Mannie's attention
flagging, we promise we'll return
tomorrow. His apprehension
still apparent, his big concern
now: "How much will this cost? I've saved
forty-two dollars. I can give
it all to Luis." "Costs are waived
for those who can't pay." Tentative,
Mannie flashes a tearful smile.
Handing him a tissue for his face,
Luis lags behind to talk, while
I move on to our next new case.
County fails people every day
but not by making poor people pay.

The second young man gazes out
the window, no disappointment
or sadness, no terror, no doubt
in his voice. "I don't want treatment,"
a Thai man, in a language I
don't know, not even *poquito,*
explains quietly. "Fate is why.
The wheel must turn three times, so
there's no need to struggle against
the revolutions of karma.
In past lives, my deeds have dispensed
with a vain appeal to pharma."
He looks at me. "Tell the doctor
no medicine, but I thank her."

The translator, also Buddhist,
had tears in her eyes, but nodded.
My inclination, to resist,
was a Western one. My God did
not respect the conjoined balance
of *chit* and *chai,* of soul and mind,
she said. Doctors' intelligence
Occidentally leaves behind
the soul. The man speaks earnestly
as though explaining to a child.
The translator interprets. "He
wants to go home, be reconciled
with his family, relinquish
this life, not painfully languish."

These words are hard for me to hear,
even harder to understand.
Lu joins up with me as I near
my office, walking outside, and
as we walk in, we talk. The wheel
turns three times, to hear, to know, to
bring that change into your life. Healing, teaching can bring the change you
have achieved to others to re-
new them. My phone rings. I'm tired, curt.
"Yes?" A female voice. "Doctor, we
need you now!" "Wait! Who are – " I blurt.
I'm ready, but she is faster.
She hangs up before I ask her.

Plague upon plagues

R emarkably, the plague TB –
tuberculosis – in decline
for far more than a century
in the U.S., took a new line
in the early 1990s.
The incidence leveled and then
began to climb. TB disease
can hit hard. Especially when
combined with HIV, neglect,
drug use or being foreign-born,
tuberculosis will affect
a whole community, suborn
its health, and sew in lungs the seeds
for decades of public health needs.

County patients are all those things:
immigrants, neglected, addicts,
AIDS infected. Then TB flings
yet more misery. It afflicts
from a distance (well, the distance
of a few feet or hours) by
air. The old barfly, for instance,
or the emaciated guy
in the jail bull pen, coughing all
night in a crowd, propels TB
into stagnant air. The germs stall,
kept aloft by apathy,
until they are, unsuspected,
inhaled by the uninfected.

Fortunately, the prognosis
for someone with TB is good.
With treatment, tuberculosis
can be controlled and cured. I would
caution, however, that treatment
requires a handful of meds
each day for the greater extent
of a year. It totals hundreds
of pills, some with bad side effects.
But if the lunger fails to take
his meds as protocol directs,
his lack of compliance may make
his bacilli drug-resistant,
his TB cure yet more distant.

Here's another category
at higher risk for TB: staff,
nurses, and doctors at County,
exposed every day. Almost half
of Chicago's nine hundred-some
new TB patients pass through these
scarred doors. The distant steady hum
you hear? Fans, dispelling TB's
wafting germs, ineffectively,
as it turns out. In my first few
months of working at County, three
nurses, one doctor, and LaRue –
a lifetime County employee –
all develop active TB.

LaRue runs the elevator,
and has exposed hundreds – BP,
staff, patients, visitors. Dr.
Boss and Occ Health nominate me
the person in charge of tracking
down and skin testing employees
who breathed air near LaRue's hacking.
At night I dream of PPDs.
Florida knows I'm feeling blue.
She leaves a present, another
stapler, this one with staples too,
on my desk. I go to thank her.
She sweetly has some news to tell:
for 3 weeks, she's been dating Del.

Every available square inch

W & C always starts,
continues, and ends with turmoil.
As I walk in, the pile of charts
foreshadows today's work and toil.
Our health system is a nightmare,
accessing AIDS care a burden.
We provide comprehensive care
for these women and their children,
using every square inch of space
to make some kind of connection:
child care, peer group, dental health, case
management, used clothes collection,
family planning, groceries,
social services, PPDs.

Inhaled pentamidine, pap smears,

legal advice, vaccination,

substance counseling, volunteers,

glasses, safe sex education,

public transportation tokens,

researchers, birth control, mental

health workers, socks and shoes, children's

crayons, hearing aids, parental

guidance, vitamins, translators,

taxi vouchers (once in a while),

snacks, GED educators,

condoms, grade school supplies, sterile

dressings, massages, compliments,

chaplains, follow-up appointments.

In clinic, we encourage all

patients not to get pregnant, not

to have a child to care for. Call

it selfish. The women have got

to care for themselves first. This, plus,

if one gets pregnant, she has had

unsafe sex, quite possibly thus

infecting her partner. A sad

third consideration for these

women: thirty per cent of their

kids get HIV, a disease

to which no one's child should be heir.

Based on the number of kids who

come here, the word didn't get through.

We provide childcare in clinic
so the moms can see their doctors.
AIDS clinic kids – cacophonic,
personable numerators
in the HIV equation –
eat popsicles, color rainbows,
make their visit an occasion
to have a party, not the "woe's
me" day their mothers make it be.
Today, the kids dance, gyrating.
to an Ella Jenkins CD
around the reporters waiting
for Big Possum, scheduled to do
a press conference here at 2.

I find BP in my exam
room, smoothing his hair in the mirror,
in retreat from hallway bedlam,
unguarded, almost sweet, sincere.
His smile, as I catch him preening,
is sheepish, even embarrassed.
"Mr. Poisson, I've been meaning – "
"Call me BP." I look aghast.
He quickly adds, "everyone does."
I remind him he needs a skin
test for TB because he was
exposed to phthisical LaRue in
the elevator. Patiently,
BP submits his arm to me.

At the press conference, BP
describes, grandiosely, his plan
to "optimize community
HIV care in clinics." Fran
grumbles in the back. BP takes
the credit, while she does the work.
Like her rival, BP, she aches
to be important, a shared quirk.
The plan is really nothing new,
just proverbial deck chairs on
the Titanic. "That's all, thank you."
Fran's hand shoots up. "Mr. Poisson?"
Reluctantly, "Yes, Doctor?" "Your
cousin, the Board Commissioner?

"Did he vet this plan with you? Did
you clear it with him first?" "Doctor – "
She spews venom. His carotid
pulses against his jaw. Bitter
words spent, Fran concludes, "Well, did he?"
"Is that your question, Doctor?" "Yes!"
"No, he didn't, Doctor." BP
turns to leave, then says, "I'd address
the rest of your comments but now
is neither the time nor the place."
He steps down. Fran doesn't see how
much he's gained – while she has lost – face.
Grace goes with him, apologetic,
then returns, unsympathetic.

"Fran, what were you doing? Really,
Fran, what? You're too old for tantrums.
This isn't about you or me.
It's about our patients. It comes
down to humility, learning
that turf, your budget, your ego
mean nothing to someone yearning
to live to see her daughter grow,
someone ashamed of HIV
knowing she's dying but hiding
all that fear from her family.
She comes here, alone, confiding,
only to find you and BP
squabbling over County debris."

Fran claims unrepentance. "He's a jerk."
But I think she's feeling abashed.
First Grace, then Fran, return to work.
This isn't the first time they've clashed.
I try to set the scene for Will
over shrimp and grits at Wishbone.
BP, dogged, battling uphill.
Fran, belligerent, bitter, prone
to venting the frustration we
share, but in the wrong direction.
Crowds of women with HIV,
balancing life and infection.
"There's no excuse for this mess. It's
health care managed by idiots!

It's the worst hospital ever!"
Will asks, "Yes? It's where I would go
if I were sick." I had never
thought about that. His CBO,
ArtsLaw, is a small non-profit,
too small to buy health insurance
for the staff. They can't afford it.
To County's tempest-tossed immigrants,
black people, outcasts, add one more
group, the uninsured, to those who
seek relief at its crumbling door.
With time, I'll learn it's not rare to
take care of a Northwestern grad
whose luck has turned from good to bad.

Will tells me he was convinced he
should be a starving painter. "I
wanted to be the next Hockney,
without his talent." "Is that why
you became a lawyer instead?"
"Eventually. I was half
way through art school before I said
'what am I doing here?'" We laugh.
"I like law, but it's contentious.
I miss painting's quiet center.
Law's like…what's your word? Tinnitus?"
Backtrack a moment, in case you're
wondering: BP's PPD?
Negative. No sign of TB.

David Tweedle

David Tweedle, forty-seven,
a gay man, singer, baritone.
Late AIDS, helper cells eleven.
Chronic dementia, cause unknown.
Opera buffa, once so funny
Malatesta fame was slated.
Now he has run out of money,
bank account evaporated.
His salt-and-pepper beard grown wild,
David sits in a recliner.
His onetime (but not now) beguiled
true (interior designer?)
love never visits, never calls,
afraid to venture County's halls.

At County, in-patient charges
are fully covered, perversely
(even as the cost enlarges),
while out-patient bills, conversely,
are not. Public payers won't pay
for care delivered at home. For
this reason, patients sometimes stay
"in house" for days and weeks (or more)
waiting for obscure therapy
or hospice care, a derm or psych
consult, ECT., or drugs we
can't provide to outpatients, like
home IV antibiotics
or palliative narcotics.

Dave is waiting out his second
week here while we try to schedule
a CT. Ward nurses are fond
of him because polite words spool
from his mouth, an endless loop caught
in his mind. "Thank you. Gee, that's great.
How do you do?" His line of thought
resembles more a figure-eight.
When you wake him: "How do you do?"
And when you ask him how he is:
"Gee, that's great." Does this hurt? "Thank you!"
Crumbs from his thoughts' agenesis.
Meanwhile, David takes up a bed
that someone else could use instead.

Mannie improves and we transfer
him to the AIDS Ward where, each night,
he cries to himself. We refer
him to Psychiatry. This might
have helped if the intern they sent
spoke Spanish but she didn't know
mierde. She asked what a proverb meant:
"Now, Emanuel, what does 'No
moss is gathered by a rolling
stone' mean?" Mannie pulled the bed sheet
over his head. No cajoling
would inveigle him to complete
her questions. Her diagnosis?
Major depressive psychosis.

Luis and my diagnosis? She
is clueless. With Mannie's consent,
we ask his priest to stop to see
him, and begin antidepressant
meds. Later, Mannie asked Luis:
" ¿This 'moss,' *hay mosgo, justo?*
So why was she talking to me
about moss, man?" "*Está loco,
hermanito.*" Luis treats him
like a kid brother, gently jokes
about his hygiene, makes him trim
his nails, brush his teeth, tries to coax
him to eat with cold Jarritos
and *barbacoa burritos.*

When the Ward is short-staffed, Big Nurse
pitches in, which is how she hears
Mannie crying. Though starched and terse,
she warms to him. Maybe it's tears
which move her. Mannie, for his part,
becomes attached to her, because…
because I don't know why. "The heart
has reasons which the reason does
not understand." One day, she brings
him a stuffed toy, a tiger. She
cooks him Filipino dumplings.
After discharge, stopping by, he
brings Big Nurse a box of Fannie
May. "*Gracias*, Miss B! Mannie."

Chicago, known for big shoulders

Chicago, known for big shoulders,
sometimes also has a big butt.
BP sits on his, slaps folders
angrily around his desk. "What
does she gain by trashing me?" Fran
has been interviewed – again – by
the Tribune about BP's plan
to optimize clinic care. "'I
am dismayed, particularly
by Mr. Poisson's ignorance
about the AIDS community.'
Campion doesn't miss her chance
to publicly disgrace me, which
is why I've had it with that bitch."

BP has nursed this grudge for years
ever since Fran called him a stooge
of the Board. Each time she appears
in the news, he gets a deluge
of bad press. On his leatherette
throne, finger tips touching, lips pursed,
he studies the clinic's budget,
examining the funds disbursed,
looking for clues bookkeeping's lax.
"Soap! Condoms! Sunflower seeds! Who's
authorized purchasing snacks?
Crayons! Groceries! Socks and shoes?
Is she running a clinic or
stocking a Family Dollar Store?"

Clinic is held in a lean-to
appended to the Beaux Arts heap.
It's as if they didn't mean to
build something they wanted to keep.
The clinic has a rhythm, which I
have settled into. Greetings all
around, chitchat, check the supply
cart and restock if needed, call
my first patient's name. Heads down 'til
all the patients have been seen, then
debrief on problems with Fran, fill
out paperwork, forms. It's often
8 pm before we're finished,
tired, out-of-sorts, and famished.

Today I've got a full roster:
18 scheduled, a few walk-ins.
The first, Dawn, has shingles (zoster),
a blistering red rash. Her skin's
oozing and she can barely deal
with the pain. We should admit her. She
has no one for her kids, though. She'll
try staying at home and we'll see.
My next patient's teeth are loose and
rotted. They clack around like dice
in a cup; one hangs by a strand.
Crack – rock cocaine – exacts this price.
Nothing – *nothing* – matters to an
addict but crack. No thing, no man.

I've talked Rox into rehab twice.
Each time she absconded, hating
the "shibby foo' an' bab abvithe."
They've put her back on their waiting
list, but I know they won't give her
a third chance. She bolts when I go
out to get our drug counselor,
racing off to score crack or blow.
Next up: Joyeuse, who, in Haitian
(with high school French, I can almost
grasp) pushes for information.
Her eight year old, she likes to boast,
loves school, takes her medicine on
time, doesn't flinch when blood is drawn.

Because of this, Joyeuse expects
her to become a doctor. Could
I recommend some school subjects
for her daughter to study? Should
she get extra work in science
or math? Joyeuse's fixation
seems premature. Her impatience,
though, reflects her situation.
Joyeuse, her daughter, and a son
all have advanced AIDS. I suggest
that her daughter play, laugh, swim, run.
At this age, these prepare her best.
"*Non, non*, doctor, you no *konprann.*
Souple, ban mwen a leson plan."

My fourth patient, Lunelle Jones, just
moved back to Chicago from South
Carolina. Lunelle's robust
and talkative, a motor mouth.
She was diagnosed in L.A.
in 1990. CD4
count? She's not sure. She's going to stay
at her sister's house in South Shore.
AIDS defining illnesses? Oh,
no, nothing like that. She tells me
she hosted a local cable show
in Charleston about HIV
I'm impressed – it takes guts to go
public with AIDS. She's a hero!

She smiles modestly. She did not
bring health records from her prior
doctor in Charleston. She forgot.
That's no problem. We require
all new patients to have baseline
AIDS tests (Western blots), CD4
cell counts, and PPDs. I sign
the order, send her out the door.
Blood tests are drawn on the second
floor in the Central Lab. I'm pleased
to meet Lunelle. She's a seasoned
AIDS activist, seems to have breezed
through the sometimes difficult trans-
ition to a new doctor's hands.

Midway through the afternoon, Fran
with Grace, is summoned to BP's
office. Cassandra, veteran
of their tug of war, tries to ease
my mind. "He's gonna chew her ass
and then send 'em back with their legs
between their tails." Huh? Okay, Cass.
Meanwhile, if one more patient begs
me for narcotics…a chronic
problem: drug seeking behavior.
Fran and Grace limp back to clinic
at 6. "BP found fault with our
accounting," Grace says with a frown.
"He's decided to close us down."

A little mouse in no hurry

J acek spoke Polish when he spoke.
He didn't speak very often,
his speech quelled by – perhaps – a stroke.
Jacek's Polish nurse could soften
his face, singing a nursery song.
"Uciekaj…myszko…do…dziury,"
Jacek would sing, stumble along.
A little mouse in no hurry.
Jacek's here to evaluate
his right-sided paralysis,
but he has had to wait…and wait.
CT scans, done on the basis
of need with one machine. An end-
stage AIDS patient? Hard to defend.

Jacek's large family takes turns
by his side. They feed and dress and
bathe him, and Elzbieta learns
all their names. Rosary in hand,
his mom murmurs in Polish. She
doesn't know — at least no one told
her — that Jacek has HIV
Around his neck she tied fivefold
healing scapulars, so perhaps
she knows after all. In a wheeled
chair in the center aisle, he naps.
The steady stream of people yield
like a river around a stone,
his mother's prayers the undertone.

Mannie has been readmitted
with bacterial pneumonia,
his bedside table outfitted
with a photograph, gardenia
in her hair, of Big Nurse. This seems
curious to me, and I ask
"A photo of Big Nurse?" He beams,
talking through the oxygen mask.
"Nah, it's a picture of my mom.
She looks like *Señora* B!" Now
I can more easily fathom
his affection, given the pow-
er of a mother, whether real
or surrogate, to calm and heal.

County belongs to the public

Women and Children's clinic, near
seven. We've worked since noon and still
have piles of charts in the rack. Here
the AIDS epidemic's uphill
fight is measured in the number
of new patients each week: three, ten
eighteen, twenty. I remember
the first time I heard of AIDS. Then –
10 years ago – I wasn't prescient.
I had no idea that thousands
were infected in the nascent
epidemic. Now it expands
faster than we can find space to
file patient charts as they accrue.

Which is partly why the clinic's
planned closure has sparked an uproar.
"County leaders schizophrenics!"
bays the Defender's editor.
"Closing clinic as AIDS cases
explode!" BP fights back. Quoted
in the Sun Times: "I've found traces
of fraud, improper and bloated
spending." BP has given us
six months to transfer our patients
to other clinics. We discuss
and plan at weekly meetings. Since
Fran's outburst, she and Grace have warred,
making clinic tense and awkward.

Last week, Lunelle finally stood
in line at the second floor lab
and got some – well, one – of the blood
tests I had ordered. Her confab-
ulation – "You didn't order
an HIV test!" – puzzles me.
Fortunately, her T-helper
cell count is normal. I'm happy
that her immune system's still strong.
Lunelle comes to clinic every
week. She's found a place to belong.
When she hears the clinic will be
closed, she starts a petition drive
to keep "my AIDS sisters alive."

I hadn't seen Cherie for months.
Today, she brought her pill bottles,
completely full, all six at once
with dates from last year. She bristles
when I ask if she is taking
her medication, starts to cry,
big sloppy sobs, shoulders shaking.
"I don't know when to take it. I
can't keep all those instructions straight."
"Cherie, it says right here. 'Take two
at least one hour'" – I demonstrate
by shaking two out – "'before you
eat or two hours after each
meal.'" I glance up to gauge my speech.

Her tears are angry now. "What do
you want? I can't read, never could.
I never learned." "You can't read?" You
can't read. I didn't know. I should
have thought of that. She has taken
forms home rather than sign them here
and said that she had "mistaken"
one word for another. I fear
I haven't recognized other
patients – the older woman who
holds 'scripts upside down, another
who always makes a big to-do
of "weak eyes" – who can't read. "Cherie,
I didn't know. I am sorry."

The kids' rainbow drawings are taped
on my exam room wall. Musing,
a solution comes to me, shaped
by their artwork. I draw, using
a Women and Children's crayon,
the blue and white at grinning noon,
the red pills with the waking sun,
the green one at the rising moon.
I struggle with the depiction
of pre or post prandial, and
Cherie selects, with some friction,
a drawing of fork and plate, spanned
above with the word "or," tablets
to left and right, framed by brackets.

"I need to teach you the word 'or'.
I don't want you to overdose
or take it at the wrong time." "You're
not going to!" Cherie leans close.
"All you people want me to read.
I don't want to. Leave me alone!
You think that I should be pitied.
You think you're throwing me a bone.
I don't want your fucking bone, your
letters, your reading." She is wild
now, swears when Grace comes, slams my door
and leaves angry, grasping my child-
ish drawing, I hope compliant,
but not reading, still defiant.

Will and I have gone out for Thai,
gone to the Chicago Film Fest,
picked apples and made apple pie,
and just last week, at the Park West,
saw Poi Dog Pondering live. This
evening, though, I'm so tired, so
sick I can barely move. We'll miss
the opening night of a show
for an ArtsLaw group. "There's no one
I'd rather miss it with." Will brews
me tea with honey and lemon,
and reads while I doze off. My bruis-
ing call schedule will relent for
March, then back on consults once more.

During my weeks off service, I'll
write grants for research funding, catch
up on dictating charts (the pile
is reaching the second floor), match
my socks, maybe go to the gym.
I am looking forward to time,
unmapped, with Will. When I'm with him,
life makes sense, meters scan, words rhyme.
One Sunday afternoon, he shows
me how to paint. My face, mirrored,
my subject; my style, proto-van Gogh's.
But we have fun, ending up smeared,
laughing. Mars yellow, cobalt blue,
Cherie's anger a dimming hue.

County belongs to the public,
and therefore public mores prevail.
This sometimes makes for symbolic
stances and attitudes which fail
to realistically address
our patients' medical needs. My
case in point: abortion. Access
to abortion is narrowed by
Medicaid, which only permits
abortion when the mother's life
is put in danger. This limits
the options, not exactly rife
to begin with, for women who
are poor, pregnant, and have AIDS too.

Shanti comes to the clinic when
she is twelve weeks pregnant. Living
on the street since the age of ten,
she is semi-feral, starving.
She has traded sex for drugs – crack
cocaine – food, and a place to crash.
She was tested at The Way Back,
a shelter for street teens. A rash
alerted a counselor to
the dismal possibility
that she had AIDS. When tested through
County's outreach program, Shanti
was positive for HIV,
hepatitis, and pregnancy.

Hospital administration
denied Fran's request to permit,
for Shanti's sake, an abortion.
Today, her first clinic visit.
Sharon Price, our OB/gyne
physician who specializes
in pregnant teens with HIV,
takes on Shanti's care. She sizes
Shanti up and anticipates
trouble. But Sharon has a plan.
If she (Shanti) participates
in a study, she (Sharon) can
get extra resources to try
to assist Shanti to comply.

County is part of the AC
TG, the AIDS Clinical Trials
Group, a nationwide HIV
cooperative which compiles
data from many clinicians.
ACTG, among others,
studies infants' acquisitions
of HIV from their mothers.
 The study that might help Shanti
is Zero-7-6. Pregnant
women take oral AZT
starting at 12 weeks. The moment
a mom goes into labor, she
gets the AZT by IV.

The baby, once born, gets the same
in syrup form for 6 weeks, then
is followed for 6 months. The aim
of the study: to determine
if this prevents AIDS transmission
from mother to baby. To test
this conjecture with precision,
a placebo-controlled trial's best.
Sharon and I try to explain
this to Shanti. "We won't know if
you get, by mouth and then by vein,
medicine or sugar. The difference is hidden. We don't know,
you won't know, if it's placebo.

"We don't know if AZT's safe
in pregnancy. We don't know yet
if it works – " Shanti starts to chafe –
"to prevent infection, or get – "
"You don't know shit, do you?" Shanti
snaps. I have to turn away to
hide the smile that shows I agree.
Shanti consents to enroll, through
County's ACTG. The case
managers arrange monthly WIC
checks, bus pass, Medicaid, a place
to live. The carrot, not the stick,
we hope will keep Shanti on track,
safely pregnant, away from crack.

Shanti is not a nice person.
I wish I could say that she cleaned
up, that she behaved no worse than
most teens, that when we intervened
she turned her life around. But that
didn't happen. Shanti is young,
selfish, addled by drugs. She spat
at Cassandra, the desk clerk, swung
a baby doll manikin at
the teacher in her parenting
class, lost clumps of hair in a cat
fight after slyly tormenting
a girl at the shelter for days.
How could she keep a child to raise?

Ramadan

The USSR had its fill
of communism but County's
socialist comrades never will.
The old guard Communist Party's
still loitering here. The local
cell's fearless leader? Dr. Marks,
my ID colleague. His vocal
dialectic rarely strikes sparks
these days. I've seen idealists
age in different ways. They become
glum or withered or arsonists.
Some curdle like Dr. Boss. Some –
Marks – rally at noon each Tuesday
in a revisionist display.

In the park across the street from
County some dozen people meet
this week to shake their fists and thumb
their noses; much less light than heat.
Their usual demands? An explanation for and an end to
sickness and poverty, subjects
which rouse ardent Reds but tend to
make the County proles fall asleep.
Comrade Marks, taking charge, inflames
the small group's senses, his voice leap-
ing through the bullhorn that he aims
at Administration's windows.
Pigeons scatter as he bellows.

I hear their thrum as I sit through
a stultifying lunchtime talk
on kidney stones by Dr. Chiu.
The room overlooks the sidewalk,
Harrison Street, and the park. Their
theme today, the pending closure
of W & C. "Health care
is a bankers' plot. To insure…"
My eyes close, my mind gathers wool.
The next voice sounds familiar. What
do you know! Lunelle Jones, with bullhorn in hand, leads a chant. "Don't! shut!
us! down! Don't! shut! us! down!" echoes,
the park pigeons' manifestoes.

ॐ

A number of the residents
are observing Ramadan. They
fast from sunup to sundown. Hence,
they get testy late in the day
as rounds drag on and hunger bites.
I try to fast but only make
it – barely – to lunch. On some nights
we've gone together when they break
their fast at Reza's, a Persian
hallal place. Tariq and Teslam,
on rounds, share a pocket version
of the five pillars of Islam:
faith, meditation, charity,
discipline, committed journey.

The residents invite me to
Eid ul-Fitr, celebrating
the end of Ramadan. "*Eid Mu-
barak!*" The house is vibrating
with party goers' revelry.
Children, in their fancy clothes, race
around the room, stopping only
when swept in an adult's embrace.
Dr. Qot, the chief resident,
plays the charming, solicitous
host for this holiday event.
He points out his own boisterous
daughter and son, Amira and
Khan, running with a rowdy band.

Residents, usually so
careworn and composed, are happy
and relaxed, their faces aglow,
the holiday their therapy.
I meet wives and husbands, parents
even – Radu's mom, Tariq's dad,
proud of their children's achievements.
Interns, instead of mulling bad
lab results or IV fluids,
reminisce about iftar treats
their mothers made when they were kids:
coconut dates, sesame sweets.
Although it's cold, some of the men
stand outside, grilling lamb, chicken.

The evening is winding down when
Dr. Qot, concerned, asks me to
look at his daughter. The kitchen
resonates with women. A few
are sitting with Amira and
her mother, who holds the girl, just
recently racing. A wet strand
of hair crosses her forehead, clust-
ers of tiny blisters scattered
on her skinny arms and flushed face.
I ask her mom, as if it mattered,
about exposures, but her case
is so typical of this age:
chickenpox, easy to manage.

She'll be fine. I give Dr. Qot

and his wife some suggestions to

help their daughter feel better — oat-

meal baths, Tylenol — and review

what to watch for. Our residents

are from the subtropics. Chicken-

pox is rare in warm climates. Since

they haven't studied or taken

care of patients, they wouldn't know

what to expect. Worse, far worse: most

have not *had* chickenpox and now

residents, families — almost

all — were exposed. Celebration

becomes contact investigation.

David and Jacek

The nurses on the AIDS Ward have
Dave and Jacek in chairs in sight
of the nursing station's desk. Dave
leans leftward and Jacek leans right.
We've been calling Dave "Tweedle Dee"
while we call Jacek "Tweedle Dumb."
Our humor is cruel, I agree.
We laugh so that we won't get numb.
One nurse made a leash, a tether,
out of gauze and several bed sheets,
then she tied the chairs together
so the two doze in tandem seats.
Dark David: large, benevolent,
noisy. Blond Jacek: slight, silent.

When awake, the men push their feet, so
they circle clockwise as a pair,
traveling up and down, in slow
spirals. Each man seems unaware
of the other. They pivot
up to the rounding team – "Thank you!" –
in the Ward's center aisle. "Move it!"
commands Big Nurse. "How do you do?"
David chatters as they swivel
through. Patients, killing time, place bets
on how far the two will travel,
using pennies or cigarettes
(legal tender of wards and jails)
or jello cups if all else fails.

Mrs. Gladys Knight has me in
her sights from the Ward's other end.
Her watery eyes, doughy skin,
forward leaning shuffle, which tend
to result from a lifetime's worth
of anti-psychotics, tell me
things her memory can't unearth,
some fragments of her history.
Mrs. Knight is sixty-six or
sixty-seven. Today she thinks
seventy-six. She's lost all four
fingers on her left hand. She blinks
when asked how she lost them. "Maybe
frostbite?" she asks hesitantly.

She's also hazy about how
she got AIDS. She's one of dozens
of older patients we have now,
overlooked senior citizens
who comprise another sliver
of this outbreak. "Yes, Mrs. Knight?"
"Grace hasn't visited. What's her
problem?" In her undamaged right
hand she holds a dog-eared sheaf. "She's
always come to see me before."
Grace visits W & C's
patients when they're admitted. "You're
nice enough, but you're not Grace." Lu
and Grace are who people cleave to.

"I know she's been working very
hard, Mrs. Knight." We part to make
way for David and Jacek. "Gee,
that's great," David burbles. "I'll take
Grace your forms," I say, "if you want."
Grace has been working hard, scrambling
to keep the clinic open. Grant
writing, lobbying. She's gambling
that if she finds outside support,
BP will rescind the closure.
So far, she's received no comfort –
or money. Mrs. Knight, unsure,
distrustful, clasps her papers close,
shuffles away, tardive, morose.

This morning things are looking grim

Rodney has advanced HIV,
recurrent pneumonia, severe
diarrhea, new CMV.
His t-shirt reads "Proud to be Queer."
Each day when we see him on rounds
he has dwindled, wasting away.
He weighs less than 70 pounds,
has countless bowel movements a day.
A rectal tube is inserted
to collect the watery stool.
Fervently Rod reasserted
his desire to fight – "Who'll
take care of my cats if I die?" –
as each day he barely scrapes by.

No beds open on the AIDS Ward
so Rodney stays "on the floor." He
sulks and frets. "I'm being ignored."
Drenching night sweats develop; we
try to work up the cause and get
an electric fan to cool him.
Each day Rod says, "I'm not dead yet."
This morning, though, it's looking grim.
His blood pressure's dropping, he's non-
responsive. Dr. Suseno,
the ward intern, peels and sticks on
cardiac leads. A volcano
of vomit disrupts her routine.
She draws back then starts some saline.

The EKG shows a flat line.
Dr. T. Patil calls a code.
"Code ninety-nine! Code ninety-nine!"
Out of nowhere, people explode.
Orchestrated chaos ensues.
An intern gives adrenaline
IV. A stream of paper spews
out of the EKG machine,
heaping in white loops far, then near.
Anesthesia intubates. Jack
applies the defib paddles. "Clear!?"
Dr. M. Patil jumps back,
and accidentally catches
the rectal tube, which detaches.

The loosened end of the tube arcs
through the air to land on the fan.
Instantly, a spray of stool marks
the walls, residents, and chaplain.
Rod is pronounced dead. Eleven
people are spattered with vomit
and stool, and it's not yet seven
am. The soiled people submit
to the charge nurse who tries to clean
them up. Just Mabley, her Highness
the ward clerk, strolls down to the scene.
"Hmm, hmm, hmm! This sure is a mess,"
she says with an appraising eye
but indifferent tone. "My, my, my."

Her cool clashes with our alarm.
During Rodney's code, an intern
got a needle stick in her arm.
Dr. Suseno, her concern
wild on her face, has been exposed
to Rodney's blood and therefore to
AIDS. Occupational Health's closed
at this time of day, so a few
fellow interns hustle her, at
a trot, to the ED where she
is evaluated by Matt
Ficoll, a new doc. Policy
dictates a baseline HIV
test and then starting AZT.

AZT – the same medicine
our patients take. A few studies
suggest that, if stuck, you begin
to take it right away, your body's
more likely to subdue and clear
virus before it can infect.
Some residents and interns fear
needles so much that, to protect
themselves, they carry AZT
always, almost talismanic.
If stuck, most react evenly;
the risk is quite small. Some panic,
like a wasp's in their underwear.
Some – Dr. Suseno – despair.

Four residents and two interns
have come down with chickenpox; three
more are furloughed (exposure earns
them a few days off, until we
see if they get sick). Short-staffed as
a result, the residents' and
interns' usual hard work has
gotten harder. My team's unmanned –
it's just me doing consults. (That's
okay; by myself it's quicker.)
We find a home for Rodney's cats:
PAWS takes them in. Mannie's sicker.
He went home after pneumonia
but bounced back with diarrhea.

Dr. Suseno, tears blurring
her eyes, comes by to talk to me.
Due to her needle stick during
Rod's code, periodically
over the rest of the year she
must be tested for AIDS before
Occ Health can say with certainty
that she's not infected. What's more,
the AZT nauseated
her. She stopped it after a few
doses. Her fear, unabated,
consumes her. "I almost called you
at 3 am. I was sweating,
couldn't breathe. Could I be getting….?"

It sounds more like anxiety
attacks to me. I reassure
her, suggest a variety
of mental health referrals. "You're
going to be okay, Dr.
Suseno, but I think you need
some emotional support." Truth or
lie? Did I willfully mislead
her? Do I know she'll be okay?
I learned long ago: resilience
takes its strength from hope. To relay
strictly statistics and science
is to ground hope's fluttering bird,
leave its restoring tune unheard.

Dr. Suseno agrees to
call a counselor. She'll stop by
to let me know she's followed through.
After the initial outcry,
the commotion about closing
W & C quieted.
Administration resumed dozing.
Lunelle Jones claims she rioted
in South Carolina for new
AIDS funding, and offers to start
a small disturbance. No, thank you,
Lunelle. Finally, with stalwart
Del's bargaining (plus some bedpans),
David and Jacek get their scans.

Jacek's head scan shows a tumor
on the left side of his brain, near
the speech center. I'm in favor
of a brain biopsy, to clear
up any last uncertainty
about the cause, before we
start treatment. Jacek's family
agrees with that plan. Whether the
tumor proved by a biopsy
could be cured – well, no one expects
it will. Dave Tweedle's head CT,
done after 6 weeks here, detects
hydrocephalus. We will drain
the excess fluid from his brain.

Both need neurosurgery, which
is scheduled every third
Thursday. An unfortunate glitch
(the elevator's down) deferred
surgery this week. With Christmas
and New Year's coming up, fiscal
quotas for January, plus
staffing, neuro and critical
care bed shortages, a March date
is set. They can't go home or they'll
lose their place in line. "At this rate,"
Lu says, "at the pace of this snail,
they'll be old men," an unlikely,
but happy fate, ironically.

Christmas party

S unday morning, on rounds early,
snow falls evenly on the ground.
Opalescent. Muffling. Pearly.
Dampening harsh urban sound,
covering the blood stain pennants
on the curb outside the ED,
Saturday night's rusty remnants
of the "Knife and Gun Club" party.
This afternoon, the combined AIDS
Services' – Consults, Ward, Clinic –
Christmas celebration invades
our office. Only a cynic
would fail to be charmed by the plain
but heartfelt way we entertain.

Patients, nurses, doctors, and staff
mingle over punch and cookies.
Dr. Marks greets guests. "On behalf
of County's Infectious Disease
division, I welcome you. I'd
like to make just a few comments
on capitalism's worldwide
conspiracy. Bourgeois segments…"
Someone ups the boom box volume.
He's drowned out by Run-D.M.C.'s
…*Santa's a player, his elves joom.*
…*He bringin' me a 100 Gs.*
Kids from clinic, drunk on Fanta,
maul Luis, disguised as Santa.

Ice Tray and Cheeto are Wise Men.
Wise guys really, boldly flirting
with the guests regardless of gender. It's somewhat disconcerting
to see Ice Tray. Two weeks ago,
Big Nurse threw Ice Tray off the Ward
for dealing smack. He should lie low
but no, he's back. Shanti's here, bored
and bitchy, because Sharon told
her she must. She swears and glowers.
Lunelle ambushed then buttonholed
Mannie for what seems like hours,
while she advocates opposing
Big Possum's planned clinic closing.

Grace and her daughter, Melody,
sing Christmas carols in tandem,
sweet mother-daughter harmony.
Flo and Delnor are an "item"
now. Under mistletoe, they kiss.
Two boys from W & C
are rapping *Christmas in Hollis*,
taking turns in the repartee:
…Christmas comin' to Hollis yo
…Reindeers on the roof, gettin' down
…Landlady called out the 5-O
…Santa gone, takin' shit uptown.
Some toddlers, two kids, and Shanti
drowsily watch an elf movie.

The boombox music turns bitter-
sweet. *Remember, at Christmastime,*
those who don't know What is more fit or
more replete with irony? I'm
reminded of Jacek and Dave,
twirling down the careworn decked halls —
while some have smiles — of housestaff, grave —
some have plenty — County's shortfalls.
The children, Shanti suck their thumbs.
The Christmas outside our window
Florida and I clean up crumbs.
doesn't bring joy to those inside. Snow
hides last night's bloodshed inches deep
while Shanti and the children sleep.

Florida leaves a gift-wrapped box
on my desk. A stapler! Between
tuberculosis, chickenpox,
AIDS, and clinic closings, I've been
feeling overwhelmed. Almost no
one has what they want at County –
So many tears cried, no more can flow
There's a world outside with plenty
Here, people but no food to feed
Never enough for everyone – yet
we're surrounded by what we need.
Take what you need, give the rest...Let
us show it's Christmas time again.
Use your gifts. Heal the world. Amen.

As the junior doctor, I get
to cover all the services
Christmas Day. I'd like to forget
rounds, to be home when Dad slices
the turkey. No one told the germs
that today is a holiday,
though. And infections don't talk terms,
make truces, collaborate. They
feel no spite, no ambition, no
grief. These punk microbes restlessly
(although that word suggests emo-
tion, boredom) mutate, ceaselessly
assembling their virulent snare,
RNA base pair by base pair.

Likewise, nothing slows on County's
wards because it's yuletide season.
Nature and time impel disease,
not OR schedules or reason.
Sickness does not coordinate
with calendar expectations.
Disorder's rhythms are innate,
unbound by negotiations.
The night is cold, really cold, as
I run from the hospital to
my car. Dave Tweedle's warm Christmas
wish – "Gee, that's great! How do you do!" –
contrasts with the indifference
of stars and viral variants.

Will and I celebrate New Year's
together. I tell him my aims
for March: install Shimano gears
on my bike, watch a few Bulls' games,
sleep late on Sundays, leave work each
day by 5. The free time shimmers
in my mind's eye like a lush beach,
turquoise water, suntanned swimmers.
Then, in June, for vacation, I've
been thinking about going to
Belize, to relax, learn to dive.
Luis is from Belize. "The Blue
Hole, *Dangriga, es hermoso.*
You'll visit my mom if you go."

"Will, what are your resolutions?"
Arm in arm, snow in our hair, at one
of New Year's Eve's institutions,
outdoor First Night in Evanston.
"I see how much you care about
what you do every day. You are
passionate, committed, devout
even," Will says wistfully. "Spar-
ring in court, concocting a brief
don't thrill me. I resolve – " with champagne
we kiss and toast – "new year, new leaf.
I'm going to start painting again."
Suddenly shy, I ask if he's
considered painting in Belize.

A new year, new leaf

This morning, a group incited
by Lunelle crowded in the front
door. They clamored up the blighted
stairs to barricade and confront
BP. She had tipped off Channel
9; a reporter was on hand.
The group laid siege, their mangonel
the media. The modest band
waved handmade signs: "Save W
& C." BP was out of town
and missed the demonstration. Few
saw the late news: "Lunelle's Lockdown."
Fewer cared. Women, AIDS, a dingy hall.
It's only County, after all.

Once, County was an esteemed place,
held in high regard by patients
and public alike. The palace
of the people! Recipients
of blood transfusions benefit
from its history: blood banking
was born here. The trauma unit
is a source of great pride, ranking
among the best worldwide. Although
some may ridicule, and some feign
contempt, County's the place to go
if you're injured. This may explain
the CEO of a nearby
private hospital (a rich guy).

He's said to have a chest tattoo
(though perhaps this is a fable):
"Major trauma? Take me first to
County, transfer here when stable."
In a show of faith, Mrs. Kidd,
one of the administrators,
had her lap chole here but did
not inspire imitators.
Hypocrisy, I won't contest.
Although we believe in the work
we do, and try to do our best,
when we get sick – doctor, nurse, clerk
or Cook County Commissioners –
we see private practitioners.

The AIDS Consult Service only
has one new consult to see today. This happens uncommonly;
an easy day is overdue.
"The AIDS epidemic must be
over," Luis jokes. "The Boss must
have found a cure," I say, "and we
will have to get new jobs, adjust
call schedules, close the clinics." For
some reason, this triggers a fit
of giggles (we find our humor
where we can, remember). We sit,
laughing, while tears stream from our eyes.
Lu wipes his face, blows his nose, sighs.

The residents look on, appalled.
I know why they are confounded.
Lu has HIV, they've recalled.
Sometimes, I too am dumbfounded
at how calmly Luis persists,
with the train bearing down. Facing
the locomotive, he assists
patients, supporting, embracing.
Today he gets philosophic.
"The only thing that I'm afraid
of – it would be catastrophic
for me – is blindness." He surveyed
the group. "If I got CMV
in my eyes, that would finish me."

The residents seem reassured
by Luis's acknowledgement
of vulnerability. Moored
in our tacit enlightenment –
life is resilient *and* fragile –
doctors are more at ease, perhaps,
with embracing than denial.
"Now this new *hombre*," Luis taps
the patient's chart, "has got AIDS bad,"
and neatly changes the subject.
Myron, once – still – a nurse, has had
every AIDS expression unchecked,
from Kaposi's plummy gnarls to
CNS lymphoma, it's true.

We have time, and Myron has time,
 – since all we've got to offer each
other at this point is time – I'm
grateful he is willing to teach
the team. He patiently shows us
the chemo reservoir between
his scalp and skull. Without a fuss,
he lifts his gown, outlines his spleen
enlarged with MAC. We all percuss
his right-side pleural effusion
(Kaposi's), palpate omnibus
other findings, an intrusion
which Myron claims to enjoy. "I
like to help," he says with a sigh.

He talks about what it's like to
be a patient and a nurse. "Well,
sometimes it's okay. I know who,
what to expect. Sometimes, it's hell
because...I know what to expect."
We spend, with Myron presiding,
an hour learning from his wrecked
body. The pleasures of guiding
someone, unknowing to knowing,
sick to well, are quite similar,
like Csikszentmihalyi's flowing
experience. His seminar
done, Myron has one last point in mind.
His parting words: "Be smart *and* kind."

Although I've told Will about rounds
and consults, he still doesn't "get"
what I do. And County confounds
him. "Explain this. Why did you let
that fan blow – " "Not my fault, okay?"
He laughs mischievously. "What can
you do with three staplers?" I say
it's my dowry. "Why would they plan
to close W & C?" Yes,
that's puzzling. How do I convey
"County?" Start by showing, I guess,
to give a sense of place. One Friday
night we have made a date to dance
when finally I get my chance.

As we go out the door I'm paged
about a girl in the ED.
Our dancing date will be upstaged
unless he comes with me and we
go out after. The young woman
has lupus and is in septic
shock, probably from a urine
infection, raging, a yardstick
of how long some people wait to
seek treatment when they're uninsured.
Will is nonplussed. I sort of knew
he would be. I think he pictured
a television drama, not
County ED's frantic piss pot.

He waits at the nurse's station
once he's met the patient. I do
a thorough examination,
check the labs that are back, review
her x-rays, then talk to her mom
and the ICU residents.
In the medical idiom,
she is crashing. Her management's
now up to the Unit doctors.
They're giving fluids wide open,
antibiotics plus pressors
and supplemental oxygen.
She probably needs a Swan-Ganz.
And we are going out to dance.

I leave her mother where she's stood
all day (no chairs). Will and I go
dancing at that place on Wrightwood.
We dance in honor of Cheeto,
Mannie, Lu, Mrs. Gladys Knight,
this septic woman. *If you've got*
dreams, make them real, put up a fight
Men and women starting with not
much. The DJ's playing that New
Radicals' song *"You get when you give."*
You want to win, you got to do
You want to do, you got to live.
It don't make sense, things fall apart
Just keep it real, live with your heart.

In the morning, I go to see
her in the ICU and find
she coded, died – just 23 –
in the night. The clerk must remind
me of her name. Yet another
way in which County is different:
it's the old who die at other
hospitals. Distress apparent,
Will is shocked. I've been disabused
about immortality. I
nod to death each day. He's not used
to having people he's met die.
"But she was only 23!"
as if youth were a guarantee.

Tuberculosis quarantine

When Eugene felt better, he would
stop taking his medication.
Maybe Eugene misunderstood.
But to find the motivation
is hard when the pills make your gut
feel raw. Over the years, this had
happened half a dozen times. What
Eugene chose to ignore was bad:
stopping and starting TB drugs
almost guarantees that these germs
become resistant. Then the bugs
are much harder to treat. Alarms
sound in my head – in stereo –
when I see this scenario.

If Eugene had left visible
tracks during those years, they would criss-
cross Chicagoland. Unable
to settle down, he stayed in this
place, then in that. He slept for one
month at his mom's, six months ("too long")
at his Auntie Vi's. Charged with gun
possession ("I was in the wrong
place at the wrong time"), he spent six
months at the Jail before he got
released on bond. His appendix
was removed at Mercy. ("They shot
me up with holy water"). Yes,
throughout this, he was infectious.

"They" "pink slipped" him to Reed because
he didn't always act sane. ("Yo!
Eugene?!") Let's face it, Eugene was
a little bit crazy. Although,
if they really are after you,
it's not nuts to be paranoid.
And they really were after Eugene. He tried so hard to avoid
folks at the health department that
when they finally caught up to
him, his health records were filed at
eleven places under two
dozen names. ("Mostly Eugene, though.")
Mostly. Well hidden, even so.

The health department petitioned
the court, saying that Eugene posed
a public health threat, and motioned
for quarantine. The court imposed
admission to isolation
in The Cook County Hospital
until he took medication
and was deemed cured. Non-committal,
Eugene disappeared. Once found, he
was arrested ("Shit!") for contempt
and brought in handcuffs to County.
("Them fuckers hurt me.") We'll attempt
to treat him, although his TB
has poor susceptibility.

Eugene is now housed on TB
Isolation Ward 21.
Here rooms are private, with UV
lights, exhaust fans, doors. ("When we done
with all this?" every time he asks.)
Because he remains contagious,
we enter his room wearing masks;
visiting is an onerous
chore. His door must remain closed and
the fans are so loud that it makes
it hard to hear and understand
what he's saying. Because it takes
so much time and trouble, to be
honest, we don't see him daily.

Each day, Eugene takes 25
pills. We will treat him for two years
("Two years?! Crap.") to keep him alive.
He's stuck, until his sputum clears
(i.e., until there are no more
TB germs found in his sputum),
in isolation with the roar
of the fans, numbing and noisome.
Every Sunday, his mother packs
a lunch, rides the bus from Lawndale
to see him. And though Eugene's tracks
weren't visible, he left a trail:
TB infections, tantamount
to tracks, eleven at last count.

Camino ciego

Mannie is readmitted with
a sudden decrease in vision.
He's lost weight, lost substance, seems wraith-
like. He answers, with concision,
when asked if he can see Cheeto
across the ward, "No." "*Su cama?*"
"No." "*Mi mano?*" "*No...no.*" "*Algo?*"
"*No*...nothing." On eye exam, a
retinal specialist agrees.
Mannie has what Luis fears most:
blindness from CMV disease.
For the first time, Luis seems lost.
Mannie's decline over the last
few months has gone too far too fast.

Only one drug – ganciclovir –
treats CMV. As I write an
order, two pharmacists appear
What luck! I'll vet my treatment plan
with them. "Jean, Ed, I need to start
ganciclovir on Mannie *stat*.
Would you check the dose in his chart?"
Jean holds up a hand. Ed stares at
Jean's feet. "What's wrong?" I ask. "We're out
of ganciclovir," Jean says. "So
if we order some more, about
how long will it – " Jean stops me. "Slow
down. We don't have any drug, nor
at this time can we obtain more.

"The County has not paid its bill
to Roche for almost 3 years now.
Roche is fed up and won't fulfill
our purchase orders until – " "How
do we get some then?" I run through
all of the options I can come
up with. "The drug rep – " "Won't talk to
me anymore." "We'll borrow some
from Mt. Sinai?" Jean looks at Ed's
feet now. "Federal law prevents
that," Ed reminds me. "Do the Feds
need to know? One dose!" Jean dissents.
"Doctor, come on, it won't be one.
He'd need weeks' worth, once we'd begun."

I go to Luis's office
to tell him. Fear, anger, sadness
march across his face. Injustice
aggravated by helplessness –
that's what causes revolutions.
Fuck this. I've had it with County,
with medicine substitutions
of bad to worse, insolvency,
ego-riven management, and
criminal neglect. I thought I
could make a difference – the errand
of a fool. I give up. I'll try
to find Mannie's medication,
then submit my resignation.

Back in my office, I head for
the phone, calling the company,
the drug rep, a distributor,
then a friend at a pharmacy.
All are sympathetic and none
can help. Florida, going to
and fro, hears me – "If we had one
dose" – from the outer office – "you
could save his sight" – hears my anger
and briefly stands in my open
door. I glance up, back. "…endanger
his life, you know what will happen."
I'm storming: "We need just one dose!
One dose…" I don't even come close.

Choked, between enraged and crying,
I give up. Dozens of other
patients are still waiting – "dying" –
to be seen on rounds. I smother
my anger, gag on my despair.
I will care for those I can, let
nature take its course, then prepare
my resume and when I get
my long-awaited month off, I'll
look for a new job. I go through
the motions on rounds, all the while
mourning Mannie, my ambition to
change the world, my belief that I'd
make a big difference if I tried.

Late in the day, Delnor pages
me. "Doc, from Florida I hear
that you were rattling some cages
trying to find ganciclovir?"
"Yes, I was…but I gave up." "Well…
don't ask too many questions. I
found some." "Delnor?! You're an angel!
I'll give you all my staplers! My
eternal gratitude! Where did
you get it?" "Remember, not too
many questions. I made a bid,
called in favors, tracked some down." "Who?"
"I found a hidden cache. Immense.
On hold for lab experiments.

"Let's just say he's a famous AIDS
doctor, closing in on a cure.
It took all day to work the trades.
He had only one request. Your
month off? He wants you to take his
service in March." My month off. Time
is all I've got to trade. "He is
waiting on your answer." Sublime
turquoise waves stop rolling. Daydream
blue skies, warm beaches turn to dust
and swirl away in life's slipstream.
"Delnor, how can I thank you?" "Just
keep trying, don't give up. County
patients need you, and so do we."

Around 10 pm, Mannie gets
his first dose of ganciclovir.
To him I owe, with other debts,
the need to write what you read here.
County's stories are so massive,
so sprawling, over lives and years.
One cannot remain impassive,
yearning as the wild ride veers
to transcend this moment's weeping,
to mine some meaning more profound.
But because they are so sweeping,
because plot and theme can't surround,
these events resist their writing,
block the writer, kicking, biting.

Prodded, memories turned violent.
How to capture, without violence?
Poets write that death is silent
but activists threaten "silence
= death." I knew I had to
tell these stories, to find voices
which would contain but not subdue,
show our limits and our choices.
Finally I found the answer
when I hit on meter and rhyme.
Even then, a stern winnower
was needed. One came unasked: time.
Time fades grief, wills it: disappear.
Grief becomes grist, year grinding year.

Prose, to me, seems fully rooted
in landscape, law, and history.
Poetry seemed better suited
to love, pain, shit, and misery.
Mannie got his ganciclovir.
I gave up my month off. Either
– drug or time – can heal or hurt. Here,
however, in the end, neither
mattered. Sight, love, life death denies.
But words, though they may be fiction,
survive to log the bootless cries
of people whose lives' depiction
just begins to capture the length
and depth of their sorrow and strength.

Protest March

March's first days, like a bathtub
drained and cold after a slow leak,
feel like wretchedness at its nub.
Two clinic patients died last week.
I dreamt that both showed up any-
way for clinic today, and that
the waiting room was still. Many
women and children, peaceful, sat
in light the color and flavor
of caramel, taking pleasure in
and strength from the sun's sweet savor,
flowing warmly over their skin.
The two dead women were embraced
by all and then, by light, effaced.

Reality is neither sweet
nor liquid amber. It's hard, cold,
gray. Noise caroming off concrete.
Slush on linoleum. Uncontrolled
HIV. The clinic's looming
closure weighs on everyone in
W & C. Assuming
the timetable that the administration once announced still holds,
in a few weeks we'll need to start
scaling down. As this unfolds
we continue, each week, to chart
ever more children and women,
closing's inauspicious omen.

Shanti deigns to stop by clinic.
She talks to Sharon, says she will
stop at the pharmacy to pick
up her ACTG refill.
She's gained some weight, looks good. She throws
a fit when she hears that the wait
at the pharmacy, often close
to 6 hours, is up to 8
today. I would be indignant
too, if I were 16, homeless,
and twenty-seven weeks pregnant.
Her case manager, Dondi, bless
her, volunteers to stand in line.
Shanti smiles, her thanks genuine.

I greet Yvette, a new patient,
and usher her to my exam
room. Yvette starts out diffident
but warms up, speaks frankly. "I am
a heroin addict," she says
without apology. The skin
of her arms, cicatrixed, betrays
that fact. In recent weeks, I've been
testing a different way to take
a patient's history. "Tell me
your story." Sometimes a mistake
if it's a whining litany,
but sometimes stunning when I get
an AIDS poet. "Well…" starts Yvette.

Lunelle Jones continues to dodge
AIDS testing. "The line was too long."
or "They closed early." Her hodgepodge
excuses have planted a strong
question in my mind. Does Lunelle
really have HIV? Could she
be faking? Her fibs fail the smell
test. This poses a quandary.
Lunelle has drawn front and center
in the fight to save the clinic,
BP's sit-in's loud fomenter,
a slogan genius. It's ironic:
the person best at inspiring
is probably malingering.

Seven men in flimsy gowns crowd
the solarium shooting craps.
The players look up, briefly cowed,
realize it's me, and faces relax.
"Hi, Doc, we thought it was Big Nurse.
You want to put some money down?"
"If I did bet, I'd put the purse
on Cheeto to go home." A frown
on his pale face dampens my smile.
"Cheeto, don't you want to get out?"
The man has been here for awhile.
I didn't expect him to pout.
I had worked with case management,
found a section 8 apartment.

I thought he'd be ready to blow
this joint, but instead he's anxious.
I'm not sorry to see him go.
He's become somewhat obnoxious,
chilling around the AIDS Ward like
the 'hood. Once he started a fight,
chest prodding, raised his hand to strike,
just as Big Nurse stepped in. She might
have been seriously hurt, but
so great was her authority
that both men backed off. His slick strut,
cagey ways, and profanity,
his attitude, continue though.
I'm not sorry to see him go.

Cheeto corrals me after rounds.
"Doc, I don't want to leave. You know
all I did was drugs." His voice sounds
cracked. "I turned tricks on the down low
and I was boosting just to get
the money to shoot. Then I got
sick and had to come here. I let
that stuff go. This is the best spot
I ever been in, AIDS the best
thing that's ever happened to me.
If I go out there, I'll get messed
up again." He makes a sorry
sight, tears running down his pale cheeks, nose,
chin. I can't tell if it's a pose.

Big Nurse can tell. She walks straight toward
us, hands him a quarter. "There's a
pay phone at the end of the ward.
Here's some change. Go call your mama,
tell her to come and pick you up."
No crocodile tears for her. I
hear Cheeto catch his breath, hiccup
as he slinks to the pay phone. Sly-
ness quickly returns to his face
as he leans against the phone booth.
His voice carries from the small space;
he's not calling his mama. Smooth
as silk, he's called his friend, Ice Tray.
He sees me watching, turns away.

Will and I load bikes on Metra
on March's first spring-ish Sunday.
He's pissed off about my extra
month on service. Pulaski Day
(look it up; to explain would take
too long) gives us a chance, for one
night, to get away, for Will's sake
as well as mine. The pallid sun
doesn't warm us, but working hard
on the spring's first ride does, and we
are sweating as we turn west toward
a Lake Geneva B & B.
We're making up for days, nights lost
after my free time was "de-Bossed."

"I don't understand why that guy
would say that AIDS is the best thing
that has happened to him. And why
that woman might be pretending
to have HIV. Who would *want*
AIDS?" A cozy B & B break-
fast: tea, scones for Will, a croissant,
jam, latte for me. "It can make
life better – disability
and medical care benefits.
AIDS is an opportunity,
believe it or not, for some. It's
meaning, belonging, and structure.
Some might even refuse a cure."

We linger over breakfast, so
lucky to have bodies that move,
croissants, minds that work, espresso,
jobs we like, jam, people we love.
Meaning, belonging, structure: we're
"dissolved in something great, complete."
Time together, even a mere
overnight, makes our ride more sweet,
a spring shower less chill. We head
back to Kenosha and the train.
I've apologized to Will, said
if this night and day can sustain
us, my vacation in June is
ours, for him to be mine, I his.

Not all patients have infections

I hear a holler, then a crash.
I see the tray ladies retreat,
murmuring insults like "white trash."
I wish they weren't so indiscreet.
She is unusual in size:
large, unformed, a wild giant child.
Around her face, tangled hair lies.
Around her bed, newspapers piled.
She is raging, her breakfast tray's
contents still spinning on the floor.
I can't understand what she says.
She won't respond as I implore.
I speak slower, then louder, then
slowly, distinctly, once again.

My next thought: "she's speaking Spanish."
Remember, my skills are *muy* poor.
Suddenly, these thoughts all vanish.
She is deaf and her speech unsure.
I catch her eye and make a sign
for calm. She eyes me cautiously.
She needs a pen, motions for mine,
then writes a note furiously.
Her letters, large, unformed, like her,
emphatically spell out her need:
"GO TO THE BATHROOM, SOME WATER
TO DRINK." She hasn't peed
since yesterday, but her nurse said
"DONT GO ALONE," to stay in bed.

All night "I CALL," but, she complains,
"NO ONE HELP ME NO SLEEP JUST NAPS
THURSTY + TIRED," she explains,
scrawling sprawling words on some scraps
of yellowed newspaper. "HELP PLEASE."
I walk with her to the toilet,
wait outside the door while she pees.
I hear her drink from the faucet.
She emerges and smiles at me.
She's combed her hair and washed her face.
On the way back to her bed, we
stop to get water and replace
her breakfast tray. I write: Does she
need something else? She writes "PEPSI?"

I check her chart to make sure pop
is allowed. It is. I walk downstairs to the hospital gift shop,
little more than a stale, flyblown
newsstand, to buy a Pepsi and
a newspaper. On my return,
I pass Dr. Marks, who was standing near, talking to an intern,
during this incident. "Tut-tut."
"'What?" "Preserving the *status quo*,
the system." He runs the gamut
of socialist cant. "Don't you know
that a soda is a band-aid
on sores capitalism made?

"You should redirect her anger…"
"Dr. Marks – " "…and stand firm against
incrementalism – " "Dr.
Marks!" (He resists being silenced
when he's on an oratoric
roll.) "Dr. Marks! This lady is
thirsty. Please, stop your rhetoric
and listen. She wants one thing – ". His
look of disgust tells me I don't
get it. "A soda!" he mocks. "No!
Some respect! She's not on the front
lines of the revolution. Show
some kindness. She's a person, not
'the people,' not a bourgeois plot."

Dr. Marks opens, then closes,
his mouth, while I walk down the ward
to the woman's bed. She dozes.
I leave the paper on the scored
metal cabinet by her head,
the soda on the tray table.
I head back. Comrade Marks has fled.
It's easier, if one's able,
to talk abstractly, theorize
about remote problems than to
respond to ones before one's eyes.
Doctrinaire or doctor? In lieu
of pointless ideology,
I would rather offer Pepsi.

Fearing that he's insulted me,
Marks sends flowers, proving he knows
as much about gender as he
knows about class. But I suppose
his splenetic windmill tilting
helps him cope. I'm mulling these things,
gazing absently at wilting
chrysanthemums, when my phone rings.
I answer with trepidation.
"Now, doctor, now!" a woman cries.
This time, there's no hesitation:
I'm ready, despite my surprise.
 "Wait!" I call, trying to stop her.
In response, just the dial tone's burr.

Failing TB treatment

Eugene is failing his treatment.
His lungs sound more congested, he
has lost seventeen pounds. We sent
his germs for testing. They should be
responding to this regimen,
carefully crafted. I'm not sure
why, after something like seven
weeks of medication, his cure
seems yet farther away. We nab
his nurse: does she know what's going
on? "No idea." We repeat lab
tests and change his meds. We're blowing
our one big chance to cure Eugene.
What happens next is unforeseen.

Today on rounds, we stand outside
his room's closed door, putting our heads
together. I think out loud. "Why'd
he get worse? He's taking his meds."
Just Mabley overhears this talk.
"What makes you think he is taking
his medicine?" she asks. I gawk
at her while my brain stops making
coherent thoughts briefly. Then my
perception shifts. The most crucial –
the first question to ask – who, why,
or where is immaterial
when someone fails treatment – distills
to: "Is this guy taking his pills?"

Eugene is quarantined by court
order here on the TB ward.
Nurses record his meds, report
he takes them. Pretty straight-forward.
"Jus… Mabley, what makes you think he
isn't taking his medicine?"
Mabley says, "I asked. He told me."
This answer begs the next question.
"Why did you ask him?" "Because he
wasn't getting any better.
Eugene is my sister's baby.
I didn't want to upset her
but I've been worrying," she said.
"He's a little touched in the head.

"He told me he's being poisoned.
He spits out the pills in the trash.
No one goes in there," she reasoned,
"the residents do it slapdash,
don't take time: they in, they out, they
gone. Nurses – they *per diem*
or float – leave pills on his meal tray.
They don't care what he does with them.
It's never the same nurse twice, so
he never comes to trust 'em." I see
Eugene looking through his window
curiously. I ask if she
would accompany me – please – to
talk things over with her nephew.

We put on masks to enter. "I
didn't know," says Eugene, chastened
in her stern presence, "Auntie Vi,
that it was wrong." Mabley hastened
to correct him. "The hell you didn't,
Eugene. It's time to act grown up
and take your pills." The angry glint
in her eye makes Eugene own up
that he "sometimes" flushes the pills
down the toilet. "This doctor says
you could die, Eugene." Mabley drills
her nephew. "There ain't but two ways
out of quarantine, dead or cured.
No one wants you dead, rest assured.

"So which one is it gonna be?
The doctor's not poisoning you.
She's a good doctor." Vi Mabley
and I get a promise from Eugene: he will take his medicine
"almost always." I ask, "what would
you like to eat? What have you been
missing in here?" "Well, I sure could
use some Al's Italian beef, no
peppers." "Okay, let's make a deal.
You take your meds, and when you go
a whole week, I'll get you a meal,
a sandwich, extra gravy, and
fries – from Al's Italian Beef Stand."

Eugene's eyes light up. "Onion rings?"
We shake on it. I talk to all
of his nurses, explain that things
must be different. He must swall-
ow his meds while they watch. Because
he might "pouch" the pills in the space
hidden between his cheeks and jaws,
they should look in his mouth, in case
he still pretends. Then I go to
apologize to his aunt. "I'm
sorry. I didn't take care of Eugene. I didn't spend enough time.
I need your help to get him through.
I didn't know he's your nephew."

"Almost everbody's someone
to somebody," she says thoughtfully.
She's right. Most patients are a son
or father or favorite auntie
to someone. Shit, even the ward
clerk knows more than I do. Just when
I think I merit my Harvard
degree, I find I don't even
know what Mabley and her nephew know.
Because Eugene exposed his aunt –
when he lived with her years ago –
to his multi-drug resistant
germs, she's skin-tested. Luckily,
Mabley side-steps Eugene's TB.

∞

The big day has come, surgery
for David and Jacek! Somehow
it seems festive. Uncertainty
causes fear, while answers allow
hope – sometimes. The elevator
is working, and they leave the AIDS
Ward at 8. One indicator
of the mood: as transport parades
the men on their gurneys along
the center aisle, the others line
the way to wish them luck. The throng
disperses but for a few fine
moments it felt as though a corps
was sending heroes off to war.

Jacek will have a biopsy
of the brain to determine what
the mass, seen on neuroimagery
almost ten weeks ago, is. That
will be just the first step. Next, we'll
have to consider, if the mass
is cancer, radiation. He'll
need chemo based on tumor class.
David will get a shunt to drain
off the spinal fluid excess
that's built up pressure on his brain.
Then we'll be able to assess
if, by relieving the blockage,
we've addressed his mental wreckage.

Between the two of them, they've spent
eight-plus months here as in-patients
to get to today's big event.
The County inculcates patience.
Meanwhile, Mannie is worse. We stopped
the ganciclovir after just
five days. His white blood cell count dropped.
This side effect made us adjust
the dose, then d/c it completely.
His vision hasn't returned and
his appetite has fled. Sweetly,
his stuffed tiger and Luis stand
by his bed, urging him to drink,
to eat, not to wobble at the brink.

Now, more than ever

Now, more than ever, the two are
twins. Their crani scars and white gauze
bandages make them a bizarre
sight as they turn slowly, then pause,
inching along down the center
ward aisle in their recliner chairs.
"Thank you," David croaks. His banter
long ago stopped provoking stares.
Jacek's family wants to know
the results of his biopsy.
I do, too, to end this dumb show;
to treat and (with luck) remedy
the cause of his prolonged muteness
and one-sided paralysis.

Today on rounds, Dr. Patel,
the ward resident, reports, "Dave's
path is back, it shows PML."
"Well, that explains why he behaves…
Wait…path on Dave? Dave got a shunt.
Jacek was…had…the biopsy."
It takes a moment, then our blunt
confusion yields to clarity.
The surgeons mixed up the two men.
Names on wristbands went unheeded.
To no avail, we check again.
No. Jacek has an unneeded
shunt, his tumor isn't defined,
and Dave has lost more of his mind.

Elzbieta puts her hand to
her mouth, and turns away when I
tell her. Her shoulders slump. "Can you
help me tell his family?" My
concern is that, although they can
speak English passably well, they
may not comprehend what I plan
to say. Hell, what I plan to say
is beyond my comprehension.
We meet with Jacek's family.
Elzbieta, in translation,
first conveys my apology.
She describes, on my behalf, how
it happened, and the options now.

At first they are stunned. His brothers
pace and growl. One sister, seated,
reaches over for her mother's
hand, and says, after a heated
conversation amongst themselves,
"Thank you for telling us, doctor."
Her forthright expression absolves
me of nothing. I don't differ.
"We think it's time we took him home."
Yes, before we do something worse.
His sisters sit on his bed, comb
his hair, wash his face, while Big Nurse
tries to speed his deliverance
home. He will need an ambulance.

Since our discovery, Jacek's
deteriorated: unre-
sponsive, bedbound. BP rejects,
without comment, my urgent plea
to pay for his home conveyance.
His sisters see that he's dying
and arrange for the sacraments.
"We just want him home." We're trying.
It's Mannie, Dave, and Jacek, who
circle now, at least metaphor-
ically, spiraling down together, vying for release. For
days it's hard to tell which one's worst,
but Mannie gets to go home first.

Hansens

My beeper flashes the ED
phone number. I dial. "What's doing?"
my voice more nonchalant than me;
ED consults may mean screwing
the rest of the day. When they call
you never know what kind of train-
wreck patient awaits, what curveball
they'll pitch. It goes with the terrain.
Dr. Ficoll, my buddy, laughs.
He's used to lukewarm receptions
and half-hearted replies. The staff's
tough-skinned. ED dispositions
are chronically phlegmatic –
nothing seems to them dramatic.

146

"We've got a guy here with a weird
rash. He came from Afghanistan
5 years ago. The rash appeared
maybe a year ago. He ran
a resistance group in Helmand
in the Russian occupation.
Now he manages a newsstand
at the Kimball Brown line station."
"Okay, Ficoll, lucky for you,
we've got some time right now." I wink
at the group. "Be down in a few."
To the team, "we'll see what we think."
We finish up and head downstairs,
ready to scope the state of affairs.

I'm used to getting called about
weird rashes. Your 18 square feet
of epidermis can break out
(and does) in numerous discrete
morphologies – papules, macules,
morbilli-, licheni-, and verm-
iform, scales, vesicles, nodules,
petechiae, striae, ringworm-
iform, erosions, crusts, patches.
The body's humors use the skin –
cutaneous dots and dashes –
to telegraph the fight within,
host against germ. The bottom line?
Weird rash consults are often mine.

The ED smells smoky, but not
in the autumn bonfire sense.
Four children, cousins, have been brought
in with smoke inhalation. Tense,
sooty, damp paramedics reek
of the panicked stink of a house
blaze. We snag Matt Ficoll, seeking patient information. "How's
this rash 'weird'?" "No pigmentation
and it's anesthetic." "Huh?" "He
doesn't have light touch sensation.
Where the rash is, it's numb." "Weird!" "We
sent some labs but nothing's back yet."
He steers us toward a silhouette.

Suleiman Masood sits, behind
the drape, on one of the gurneys.
I see his features and my mind
does a double-take. His disease
is written on his brow. We shake
hands and I grasp his elbow in
my other hand. There's no mistake.
I easily feel the thicken-
ed ulnar nerve. Mr. Masood's
a dark, handsome man, leonine.
Smooth black hair, but some gray intrudes
at his temples. His eyes are keen,
eyebrows and eyelashes sparse. He
speaks some English, prefers Farsi.

A Pakistani resident
on this month's team speaks Farsi and
translates the team's questions. "What sent
you to the hospital?" "My hand
is numb. These patches of pale skin
on my chest and back…" He gestures:
who knows? On exam, with straight pin,
numbness is confirmed. The picture's
consistent: his symptoms, his signs,
physical exam, medical
exposure, and disease timelines.
Though it seems prehistorical,
Masood has Hansens, the p.c.
label these days for leprosy.

Leprosy, a word which conjures
images of nose-less faces,
finger-less hands, caricatures
now, at least in modern places.
These days, medicine – some pills – treats
Hansens, but its stigma lingers.
Mr. Masood, embarrassed, greets
his diagnosis from strangers
with downcast eyes. Dr. Saleh,
the translating resident, backs
away involuntarily,
as eons-old taboo hijacks
medical mien and discipline,
replacing it with adrenaline.

(He apologized for cringing
later. Infectious diseases
have a strange way of unhinging
those who rarely fall to pieces.)
Mr. Masood has refugee
 – not immigrant – status. He fought
the Soviets and had to flee
Afghanistan. His travails brought
recognition that we owe
the protection of asylum.
And for refugees – I don't know
why – the US, in its wisdom,
will pay all medical expense
for just one condition: Hansens.

We refer Mr. Masood to
the UIC Hansens Center.
Years later, on Devon Avenue,
I run into him as I enter
a grocery. Careful not to dwell
on his disease, I remind him
that we've met before. He is well,
smiles politely. The interim
aged him (as it has us all). He
looks less like a lion and more
like a life-battered old man. We
part. I continue through the door,
my mind tugged by the memory:
the smoky smell, shame, leprosy.

Oh vida por vivir y ya vivida

Mannie died on the Ward last night.
Luis called his mother in *Mon-*
temorelos when it got light.
Speaking softly, with uncommon
gentleness, his voice colored pink
and gray like the dawn, Luis said
her son did not die in pain. Blink-
ing back tears, holding his head
in one hand, phone in the other,
Lu told her about how fond we
had been of Mannie. His mother
should know that he loved her very
much, that he kept her picture by
his bed…here, Luis starts to cry.

Mannie's body lies in the morgue.
There is no one to release it
to. Lu and Big Nurse catalogue
and bag his belongings. I sit
at the nursing station, my mind
searching for ways to get him home.
Mannie's mother will try to find
the money, but it may take some
months. Preparing the body, a
flight to Mexico, a coffin –
it costs hundreds. His body may,
if unclaimed, end up buried in
County's potter's field, not unknown
but without mother, mourners, stone.

I call Mannie's parish church's
office. The secretary who
answers the telephone searches
the register. Yes, he went to
that church, but they have no money.
I call County's "admin of the day."
Mrs. B. stands by patiently.
"Potter's field" is all he can say.
Hesitantly, Big Nurse speaks. "My
husband, sons own a funeral
parlor in Cicero. They, I
will take care of Emmanuel,
embalm his remains, help him go
home, by airplane, to Mexico."

Listen! you can hear the roar. Lake
Michigan waves draw back, then fling.
Love and science. The give-and-take
begins, ceases, returns to bring
an eternal note of sadness.
Whether Dover or Oak Street Beach,
solace, conviction, and gladness
are always just beyond our reach.
Reason, passion, hope, despairing,
in the hospital as in life,
rock back and forth, balanced, sharing
a fulcrum as sharp as a knife.
Humbled, grateful, I nod my head.
This is how we bury our dead.

Spring returns to County. I know
because the pigeons have built nests
on the ledge outside the window
of the morgue. Beneath blue-gray breasts,
these pouters shelter two small eggs
and hope, in some passerine way,
that winter ends and its cold dregs
settle. Then hardship will segue
into spring's twitterpating light.
Reborn, innocence will flourish.
The squeakers will hatch, fledge, take flight.
Winter-processed rot will nourish
new growth. Again, the miracle
of life born from death will circle.

Del and Flo are getting married!
Noon today at the Abundant
Life Word of God Church in storied
Bronzeville. Newly leafy, verdant
patches of lawn whip by my car
window as Will and I drive down
Ashland. We're late. Spectacular
though this spring day is, our downtown
ride is a somber one. Big Nurse
asked me to take Mannie's tiger
to him. Mr. Bigayan's hearse
arrives just as I oblige her
at County's morgue. She asked me to
put it in Mannie's hands. I do.

"I do," Florida and Delnor
vow as we walk in the doorway
of their storefront church. The choir
launches into "Oh, happy day!"
In the receiving line we meet
Florida's mother, Georgia, and
grandmother, Virginia, then greet
Delnor and Florida, husband
and wife, entrepreneurial
life partners. The reception, in
the church's basement social
hall, features Georgia's fried chicken.
I introduce Will to my friends.
He shakes hands, even the Reverend's!

Dr. Boss surprises us all
by showing up mid-afternoon.
He lounges, his familiar sprawl,
in a folding chair, the table strewn
with lunch debris, then leans to tell
me: "County's an amazing place,
isn't it? You've worked hard, done well.
But slow down, this isn't a race.
Your good ideas won't run away.
We're getting a new division
member. I'm glad you're going to stay.
To start, he'll need supervision
and I know I can count on you.
You've become the division's glue."

Whether it's flattery or praise,
his words are oddly affecting,
accentuated by today's
emotions. I'm not expecting
a kind word from him. "Thank you," I
say, "It is an amazing place."
I turn away quickly as my
tears spill over, run down my face.
Will, Mr. Social, is talking
to Florida's mom, comforting
Luis about Mannie. Walking
upstairs, sorrow still contorting
me, I wander outside to find
some peace, get some air, clear my mind.

Chattering, five monk parakeets
ornament a green spring-sprung tree,
celebrating Chicago streets,
provoking an epiphany.
My present for the newlyweds?
A stapler, staples, and a gift
certificate for Bath & Beds.
We give Luis and Grace a lift
back to the hospital, stopping
on the way at Wayne's Barbecue
to get Eugene take-out Hopping
John. Today reminds me anew,
like church choirs and spring birds sing:
we must live each day rejoicing.

ACTG

Fran, Grace and I get to travel,
in May, to the ACTG
spring conference, a high level
data review held quarterly
in Washington. We arrive there
the night before the meeting starts
and meet up for dinner, to share
some Merlot and review our parts
for tomorrow's presentation.
Fran turns funny and acerbic
doing a crude imitation
of BP and his spasmodic
efforts to portray W
& C as a corrupt milieu.

Grace, although she laughs, is weary.
She and Fran have never fully
reconciled, and while Grace hoped she
could rescue W & C,
it's evident that won't occur.
Freighted by that disappointment,
Grace's mind seems elsewhere. Fran, her
face sad, makes an acknowledgment
for the first time. "Grace, I'm sorry.
I let our patients down. I let
you down." Grace doesn't seem ready
to accept Fran's apology yet.
She gets up. "I'm not feeling well.
I'm heading back to the hotel."

The next day, in a long, narrow
ballroom at the Omni Shoreham,
investigators give thorough
reports for each research program
which has been completed. Zero-
7-6 is still accruing
subjects, is still *in utero,*
so to speak. The group's reviewing
five other trials, five in which I've
enrolled subjects, so I'm eager
to see the results. For my five
patients, benefits were meager:
three are now dead, two unimproved.
I want to learn what the trials proved.

In the darkened room, aggregate
data, projected on the screen
in columns, makes me contemplate
who, not what, the raw numbers mean.
The "incidence of side effects"
means Angel, hunched in the common
toilet, heaving, crying, pale flecks –
vomit – in her hair. The anonymous dogleg in September's
Kaplan Meier plot? Bear, who died
at his parents' house, with members
of his church sitting by his side.
Eleanor's toothless grin shines through
a risk ratio and p-value.

I have the strongest feeling: Bear,
Angel, Eleanor, all dead now –
and a hundred others – are there,
are in the room with us somehow,
gliding on the projector's light
like birds on wing, not judging, just
listening from their darkened height.
I know they've given me their trust.
In turn, I've given them the best
I could, despite County's – and my
own – limitations. I've witnessed
sickness, pain, and good people die,
tried my damnedest to relieve or
cure. In short, I've been their doctor.

Jacek goes home

Jacek's brothers and sisters pooled
their funds to take him back home by
ambulance. The trip is scheduled
for today. Then things go awry.
Elzbieta comes to tell me,
"Doctor, I think Jacek is dead."
At first, I don't know who she
means, so thoroughly has he fled
my consciousness once I pictured
him at home. We go together.
He is dead. Even I, inured
to sad deaths, am sad. And whether
this will keep him from returning
home is unknown – but concerning.

Oh no. The ambulance driver
is coming down the center aisle
with a gurney to deliver
him home. With an uneasy smile,
I pull the paramedic a-
side. "This guy is basically
dead but his family wants…" "Ah…
basically?" "Well, totally…
almost…but his family would
really like to settle him back
at home before he dies. So could
you bring Jacek home, then unpack,
clean up and put him in bed, and
then call the home nurse – understand?

"Say he doesn't look good. Could you…
before rigor mortis sets in?
Look: I'll give you 10 dollars to – "
Shakes his head. "Don't even begin.
Hey, Jacek, my man, it's time to
go, your family is waiting."
He bundles him up. I go through
the motions of annotating
his chart: "discharged to home today
in…expected condition." Not –
strictly speaking – a lie. I weigh
more truth, but go with what I've got.
Jacek has spent months here, while we
betrayed Pasteur's promise, frankly.

Now he goes home posthumously.
As Jacek rolls by on his way,
David eyes him suspiciously,
yodels "Thank you!" Later that day,
Jacek's family called. "He died,"
they said gratefully, "in his bed."
Elzbieta laughed while she cried,
and then she simply cried, instead.
Dave Tweedle seems to know because
his Spirograph curves, misshapen,
meander mournfully. What does
it mean to be a doctor when
you send the dead men home and strive
to keep the living here, alive?

Shanti's baby

The people's palace? Only if
a palace resounds with the cries
of women laboring in different languages, open thighs,
in one large green-tiled room, twenty
or so at a time. Their number
is swelled today by one. Shanti
came to the ED in labor
last night, with contractions very
far apart. They admitted her
to Labor and Delivery,
where the nurses have infused – per
vein – placebo or AZT,
flowing to the unborn baby.

We don't know how much placebo
or AZT Shanti took while
she was pregnant, nor do we know
if this whole study is futile,
if AZT given like this
prevents infection in the child,
don't even know if the premise
makes sense. We don't know shit, I smiled.
By mid-morning, Shanti, effaced
and dilated, wants to push. On
her way upstairs, Sharon says, based
on Shanti's clean tox screen, we've won
a significant victory:
the baby will be born crack-free.

The whole clinic knows that Shanti
is in L&D. Midway through
the afternoon, "It's a baby!"
Cass, the clerk, shouts. In response to
our quizzical looks, she says, "I
mean, a boy!!" We cheer. "Five pounds, four
inches, sixteen ounces!" The guy
will receive sugar water or
AZT immediately.
For the next six weeks, every
six hours, he'll get AZT
syrup or a placebo. We
won't know for six months which he got
and if he's infected or not.

Shanti names her baby ShaRon.
Because the Women and Children's
Clinic is closing, Shanti's son
will see the pediatricians
in the general clinic. If
ShaRon proves to have HIV –
well, we'll have to fall off that cliff
if we come to it. Mom Shanti,
meanwhile, will be my patient in
my new clinic – I'm reassigned
to the general medicine
practice. I don't expect she'll find
her way to see me but I'll do
my best to encourage her to.

I go up this morning to give
her a follow-up appointment.
We've found a place for her to live:
a group home for teenage moms, rent-
free. Shanti's dressed in her street clothes –
she's ready to go. As she gives
ShaRon a bottle; he curls his toes
and she giggles. Their narrative's
so different from the usual
mother with newborn child, and yet
some pleasures are universal.
She lays him in the bassinette,
fondly pronouncing, "he's stone sweet."
Dondi arrives with a car seat.

Sitting at the nurse's station
on the maternity ward, I
notice that the phone extension
here is 5-3-6-5. Huh. My
office number is 5-3-6-
6. I wonder if…I wonder…
a cog turns, a tumbler falls, clicks
in place. The telephone number
here is just one digit away
from mine. Does this explain the confus-
ing calls that I get at night? Say
the nurse needs the resident, who's
sleeping in the L&D call
room, a hundred feet down the hall.

A mom, about to deliver.
The nurse, in a hurry, dials what
she thinks is the call room number,
one digit from the station's, but
she has mistakenly called me.
I walk down to the resident's
call room to check out my theory.
My investigation augments
my claim. The number here? 5-3-
6-4. That's what those calls were for!
I write up some signs: "L&D
On-Call Room: Dial 5-3-6-4."
I tape them around the station
and never get a call again.

Fools in the rain

Today ends the tenth month I've spent
on a consult service. The whole
team is female this time – student,
residents, pharmacist. The sole
exception: Luis. We decide
to make him an honorary
girl. Clothes? Hair? World view? What should guide
our prize? All seem arbitrary.
We debate: which feature confers
our femaleness? At last we vote.
We give, for dates and sleepovers,
a round pink vinyl Barbie tote.
Luis accepts with charm, aplomb.
"I'd really like to thank my mom."

Dr. Suseno calls to let
me know that her final AIDS test
is negative. She is glad, yet
for the last six months she's obsessed
about what she would do if she
seroconverted. Her career,
her health, even her family
might be endangered. Dogged fear
pursued her as if its bounty
were on her head. Her world view's changed.
Internal medicine, County –
she's forsaken them and arranged
to finish at the U of C
in otolaryngology.

With Mabley's help and rings and fries,
Eugene has turned a corner. It
turns out that high fat foods disguise
the taste of his meds and permit
better GI absorption. He's
gained weight and become a daytime
TV fan. "This Oprah Winfrey's
the bomb." Every morning, as I'm
stopping by, Eugene urges me
to watch with him. "Have a seat, Doc" –
there're no chairs, though – "Rest yourself." The
gracious host. One eye on the clock,
I stand and watch the talk show queen,
sharing her dramas with Eugene.

In mid-June, Will and I are planning a trip to Belize. Heart sore,
I've resolved to improve my Spanish as the best way to honor
Mannie's memory. I don't want
someone, a stranger, to translate
my questions, someone, nonchalant,
blasé, to hear the intimate
exchange with a patient, construe
our meaning before we've begun.
I've bought "¡*Hablar Español! ¡Sí, Tú!*"
My Walkman holds cassette tape 1.
"¡*Hola! Me llame* – " I practice.
Will interrupts me with a kiss.

On Memorial Day, it rains,
but the temperature is mild.
I get up early, while Will feigns
sleep. (I know he's faking – he smiled
when I whispered "*adios.*") We
are holding the first (and the last)
annual W & C
barbecue in Grant Park. Breakfast
on the run, lightning rounds. Quick, go
to Fran's to load her grill, swing by
Dominick's to get potato
salad and hot dogs. By July,
we'll be history. This picnic
celebrates the staff from clinic.

Fortunately, we have reserved
a picnic shelter at the Lake.
Lots of food. "No one underserved
here!" jokes Grace. Ribs, corn, salad, cake.
People brought their kids and spouses.
Will arrives right after me – he
loves rainy picnics! He rouses
teams to play Frisbee. Melody,
Grace's daughter, brought a boombox.
Summertime tunes drift, mingling in
barbecue smoke and drizzle. Docs,
nurses, clerks, our dietician
and our dentist, case managers,
W & C's caregivers.

Led Zeppelin's *Love in the Rain* blares
out of the speakers. Grace leaps
up, leading a conga line. *There's*
your love, like a light, it just keeps
burning in and out of the rain
Like stars that shine through the night
Fran Melody sing the refrain
your love leaves me breathless black white
brown Cass *breathless* the whistle blows
I run I can't stop arms milling
I'll dance in the rain in wet clothes
People *light up the love* spilling
Sharon Dondi others surround
me *light up the love all around.*

Night subdues day. More rain in store.
The children, tired, settle down.
Fireworks are promised, off shore,
later in the evening. This town
loves pyrotechnics! At the end
of next week, patients transferred, we'll
close. Patients will have to contend
with County's usual piecemeal
healthcare, calamitous outcomes –
like everyone else, traveling
from clinic to clinic for crumbs.
Already, we're unraveling.
Staff are leaving, the best ones first.
All this life, love, knowledge dispersed.

Fran and I take apart the grill,
douse the warm coals. Cassandra picks
up trash. Patients, staff, doctors will
be assigned to other clinics.
You told me that you'd never leave
me. I always thought you'd be true.
Rain, sweat, and tears mix. *Please believe*
me I can't live my life without you.
Grace rocks a sleeping Melody.
Our cleaning up pauses while we –
Fran, Sharon, Cass, Dondi, Will, me
standing arm in arm – watch Navy
Pier's blossoming showers of light
as day steals away into night.

During W & C's next-
to-last clinic session, BP
sends for Fran and Grace. Perplexed,
we speculate: what's his hurry?
Will he close us prematurely?
Cassandra shakes her grizzled head.
She believes his motive's purely
mal-intentioned. "It's like I said.
That man's heart is punitory.
He's making this hurt 'cause he can,
'cause he's the BP." Suddenly,
BP sweeps in with Grace and Fran.
For someone who avoids daylight,
he sure seems to seek the limelight.

A press conference has been set
up in the waiting room while we
worked. Dawn, Joyeuse, Cherie, Yvette,
others, watch, incuriously.
BP steps up on the small stage,
surveys the chaotic scene. I
try to read his body language,
but it's inscrutable. Nearby,
Fran looks numbed and unnatural,
as if she's mainlined novocaine.
BP announces federal
grants will allow us to remain
open. (He's forgetting that he
alleged fraud, not insolvency.)

Grace hangs back, her tired smile wry.
BP plays media ping-pong,
deftly fielding questions flung by
the clamoring journalist throng
whom he's assembled to herald
his news. The watchful staff is floored.
As blithely as it was imperiled,
W & C is restored.
Both BP and Fran have learned from
this fiasco: BP, to share
the credit – he lets Fran make some
remarks – and Fran, more self-aware,
praises BP (though her smile's tight),
the very picture of polite.

Typical County tactics, style,
I will learn as time goes on. Fake
a threat, default on a pledge, while
real people lose their lives. Unmake
the threat, backdate the check – you see,
this performance was rehearsal.
The dead still dead, the sick, sick, mostly
indifferent to the reversal.
Patients, so used to being pawns
in a struggle, respond to our
revival with "Amen!," then yawns.
The happiest person, by far,
is that stormer of barricades,
Lunelle, the AIDS patient *sans* AIDS.

Yes, Lunelle confessed, she came clean.
Craving the attention her friends
got, she kind of – she didn't mean
to lie – embellished. She contends
that some of her story is true,
except she's never had AIDS or
been out of Illinois. She knew
that, as she became more and more
caught up in the clinic protests,
that one day she would have to tell
the truth. Inspired, Fran suggests
a great plan: we'll appoint Lunelle
the clinic's Seronegative
Committee representative.

I didn't know we had one. Fran
smiles. "We do now." I could hug her!
We resume our Sisyphean
task as if we didn't falter.
Today, a stack of ten charts, new
patients waiting to be seen:
a woman with a cross tattoo,
a girl from Austin, seventeen,
and two middle-aged sisters who
drove in from Elgin. To think: I
once crowed that my job was safe, due
to AIDS, its variations. My
one-time swagger makes my skin creep.
The Elgin sisters hold hands and weep.

Grace

The seasons have come, gone. Many
have died, many remain in place.
David Tweedle, Luis, Shanti
survive. Dead: Mannie, Jacek,...Grace.
Yes, Grace. An ED doctor called
from the suburban hospital
on June's first hot evening. He drawled,
"she's quite sick: confusion, frontal
headache, fever. Sinusitis,
I think. I've ordered an x-ray.
She says you are her doctor, yes?"
I'm not her doctor in that way...
I'm really not Grace's doctor.
My role here is sad narrator.

Grace took Fran, then me, into her
confidence. Childbirth, then a bleed,
six pints of blood, months before pure
transfusions could be guaranteed.
Her HIV diagnosed when
Melody had just turned three.
Husband gone, his faults forgiven.
Her daughter was spared, thankfully.
Some years ago, Grace weighed the pros
and cons of AZT. Neither
choice appealed. In the end, she chose
against taking the meds. Either
live life each day or – this was how
she saw it – start dying now.

Grace began as a volunteer
in clinic. Soon she was hired to
manage it. But year after year,
implacably…These thoughts race through
my mind. I know he needs to be
told. Headache, fever, confusion.
If the ED doctor knew, he
might reach a different conclusion.
I speak. "Did she tell you she is
HIV positive?" Silence,
followed by "No, she didn't." His
voice resonates with annoyance.
"Well, that changes things, doesn't it?"
Yes, I guess it does. Quite a bit.

The harmonics in his voice shift
abruptly. His cockiness fades.
I now hear indifference, short shrift
for Grace. A black woman with AIDS.
Prostitute? Shooter? Who cares? He
doesn't. I try to rekindle
his interest, but for a County
doctor and her patient, it's nil
Grace will be admitted, started
on IV antibiotics.
I call Fran; she's brokenhearted.
I know their long estrangement pricks
her conscience. First thing tomorrow,
she will visit, cloak her sorrow.

In the morning, Will and I leave
for my long mused-on oasis:
ten days off in Belize, where we've
made plans to visit Luis's
family, spend time at the beach
near San Pedro, practice Spanish,
climb Mayan ruins, sleep late each
day, drink cold beer, eat lots of fish.
We fly out of O'Hare, change planes
in Houston. I call Fran. Nothing
improved, in fact, worse. She explains.
Grace's brain scan shows many ring-
enhancing lesions, lymphoma,
and she's slipped into a coma.

Luis's mom, welcoming, warm,
shows us Dangriga. On our last
day with her, a child from the *farm-
acia* runs in at breakfast.
"*Mamí, Luis* is calling for
the *gringa* doctor." *Tià* and
her son exchange greetings before
she hands over the phone. I stand
by the counter, while pharmacy
business swirls around me. Luis
tells me what I know already.
"Grace died yesterday." By degrees
this will pierce my heart, in ways that,
at this moment, I can't guess at.

Will and I thank *Tià* for her
kindness, for all she's done for us
The rest of the day's a sad blur.
We collect our things, board a bus
that rattles to Belize City.
Another bus and then a boat.
By nightfall, San Pedro, pretty
and off-season, quiet, remote.
The next morning, while the sun's still
low and small waves roll to the beach,
we set off, without a plan, Will
and I walking, holding hands, each
lost in thoughts of our own making,
San Pedro's households just waking.

Shortly after I met Grace, I
ranted to her. "How can you stand
it? County makes me crazy. Why
do you stay?" "It's a love story." And
seeing my surprise, she amended,
"Kind of a love story. Longing,
obstacles, loss," she contended.
"Partners, by turns, wronged then wronging.
Plots twist. Side narratives accrue.
At its core, passion. With luck, love
resolves into meaning. Why do
I stay? Because, like you, I'm one of
the people whom the story's about.
I want to see how it all turns out."

I laughed at her then, and she turned
away, smiling. "You'll see." And since,
I have seen. Grace was right. I've learned
enough of County to convince
me that it is a love story
about countless small devotions
and surrenders. An allegory,
like the waves of lakes and oceans:
the ebb and flow, the gift that's taken,
the ceaseless rhythm of need relieved
by love. Grace won't be forsaken
although her death is greatly grieved.
Her absence urges us, above
all else, to treat each other with love.

June's last day

We finish rounds. It's not quite five.
   Our last patient today, a black
young man paralyzed in a drive-
by shooting years ago, his back
and buttocks a mess of bedsores.
He's surly and withdrawn. I'd feel
the same. Seemingly, he ignores
my explanation of how we'll
fix this problem and prevent more.
I say we'll stop by tomorrow,
and leave my beeper number. For
a moment, he yields his sorrow.
His eyes meet mine. "Thank you, ma'am." "You're
welcome." I can't guess what you endure.

I've grown far more efficient at
rounding. The residents think I
know lots. I know why they think that.
"Dr. Patel, do you know why
I know all the answers?" "Because
you're smart?" "No! Does anyone know?"
I ask the team. Baffled, they pause,
searching their fund of knowledge. "No?
Because I ask all the questions!"
They kind of get the joke. "Thank you
for your hard work. Everyone's
invited to dinner at U-
dupi. Tomorrow, review charts
before rounds. The new attending starts."

My San Pedro tan has faded,
no sand between my toes. Dimly,
I hear ambulances' braided
wails converging on the ED
as I board the elevator
to the ground floor. "'Evening, LaRue.
You good?" "I'm great! Good night, Doctor."
His TB treatment's almost through.
The twenty-two convertors (those
infected by LaRue's TB)
completed or are getting close
to finishing their therapy.
Meanwhile, burgers and fries cajole
Eugene; Lake Michigan waves still roll.

As I walk across the parking
lot to sign over the service,
I think back on my embarking,
how much I resembled my nervous
new colleague, how little I knew
of disease, its depredations.
Find a chair, I have to tell you
about dozens of sick patients
in your trust, County's special brand
of summer, my gratitude for
this harrowing profession and
privilege, to be a doctor,
teacher, and public servant in
sweet home Chicago. Let's begin.

www.ingramcontent.com/pod-product-compliance
Lightning Source LLC
Chambersburg PA
CBHW030503260626
47157CB00005B/1626